CONFIDENTIAL
Subject: Ms. Selena Stanford

I thought my days as a secret agent were finally over, but here I am in the line of fire once again. I was minding my own business, trying to recuperate and figure out what to do with the rest of my life, when out of nowhere this gorgeous woman shows up on the doorstep of my mountain retreat! What's worse, Selena saw something she shouldn't and she's in more danger than she even realizes. I would never turn my back on my sworn duty to protect the innocent, but this vivacious lady has really rocked my world. It's so easy to lose myself when she looks up at me with her trusting blue eyes and gives me one of her dazzling smiles. I know that she's trying to be brave during this crazy ordeal, but sometimes I can sense her trembling and I long to take her in my arms and give her all the passionate reassurance she needs. But how can I do that? The last thing she needs is a bitter, withdrawn *ex*-agent to mess up her life. I've been through too much to be any good to anyone. Especially her. But once the mission is over, will I have the strength to walk out of Selena's life...forever?

MEN at WORK

MEN *at* WORK
ANNETTE BROADRICK
SOUND OF SUMMER

MEN
IN UNIFORM

Silhouette Books

Published by Silhouette Books
America's Publisher of Contemporary Romance

SILHOUETTE BOOKS
300 East 42nd St.,
New York, N. Y. 10017

ISBN 0-373-81031-8

SOUND OF SUMMER

Copyright © 1986 by Annette Broadrick

This edition published by arrangement with Harlequin Books S.A.

® and TM are trademarks of Harlequin Books S.A., used under license.
Trademarks indicated with ® are registered in the United States Patent
and Trademark Office, the Canadian Trade Marks Office and in other
countries.

Printed in U.S.A.

Dear Reader,

One of my favorite kind of hero to read about or to write about is the secret agent. Adam Conroy was an agent for years until he hit burnout and decided to retire as far from civilization as he could find.

His choice was high in the mountains near Yosemite National Park in California. However, it was obviously not far enough, because Selena Stanford accidentally found him while she was trying to get away from a mountain storm that had mired her vehicle hub-deep in mud.

It's fun to discover a self-sufficient man who is convinced he needs no one, then watch a determined woman come along in his life and point out the many errors in his way of thinking.

It almost makes me feel sorry for the unsuspecting hero. Almost, but not quite.

Hope you enjoy reading about Adam and Selena as much as I enjoyed writing their story.

Sincerely,

Annette Broadrick

Please address questions and book requests to:
Silhouette Reader Service
U.S.: 3010 Walden Ave., P.O. Box 1325, Buffalo, NY 14269
Canadian: P.O. Box 609, Fort Erie, Ont. L2A 5X3

**For Carol,
my friend for many lifetimes**

Chapter One

"What was all that hype about—that you could go anywhere with a four-wheel drive and not get stuck?" Selena looked around the interior of her Ford Bronco in disgust. "Well, I'm somewhere and I'm sure as hell stuck!"

Selena Stanford found herself in a one-sided conversation with the manufacturers of her new truck. It was too bad they weren't there to answer her.

The Bronco had slid off a steep mountain road at a curve and all four wheels were in the soft shoulder.

"You poor excuse for a mechanical mountain goat! Now what do I do?"

Her truck took the name-calling with calm

stoicism. She had a sneaky hunch the cause of her present predicament had less to do with the truck's abilities than with her inexperience behind the wheel. She had never driven on anything less defined than a carefully measured and painted street or highway.

Selena stared out the windshield in dismay. The wiper blades were unable to keep up with the deluge presently beating down. A jagged streak of lightning momentarily lit the sky, illuminating the mountainous area. The lightning was followed seconds later by a thunderous crash, graphically announcing to Selena that: one—the mountain storm was increasing in intensity; two—the rain wasn't going to let up anytime soon; and, three—the countryside illuminated by the bright display looked like nothing Clay had described to her. She was fairly certain she'd missed her turn.

In addition, she was stuck. *What a great way to begin a vacation,* she thought gloomily.

With nature's electricity gone for the moment, Selena peered desperately through her windshield, trying to see between the furious swipings of her overworked wiper blades. The feeble light of her high beams mocked her attempts to get her bearings. What had she expected to see?

Selena had never been up in the mountains of Yosemite National Park before. For the past hour she had been questioning her mental condition when she'd decided to get away from Los Angeles by herself, to camp and to commune with nature at the well-known park.

Darting light sprang across the sky once again.

If this is what it's like to commune with nature in its purest form, I don't think I'm ready for it.

The road she'd been following had grown more narrow with every successive mile and was now no more than two wheel tracks winding through the heavily wooded area. Selena had made up her mind to turn around as soon as she could find a place wide enough to do so when she lost control of the truck.

She flicked on the map light and peered at her watch. It was almost eleven o'clock. She would have reached her destination over an hour ago. Where had she made the wrong turn? She mentally reviewed the various roads she had passed but could remember no signs that would have helped her.

The thunder that faithfully followed each flash of lightning shook the truck and Selena shivered. She was not the stuff heroines are made of. She was neither fearless in the face of adversity nor willing to brave the elements under any and all conditions. In short, she was nothing like the woman she portrayed in her weekly television series.

She gazed at the dense woods around her but could see nothing that might suggest there was anyone nearby. No cars, no lights—nothing but pouring rain.

Selena ran her hand through her shoulder-length, blond hair and sighed. She couldn't sit there all night.

With fresh determination, Selena shifted the gears of the truck and began the rocking movement that should have freed her. Instead, the truck sank deeper and ominously began to tilt downward. It suddenly occurred to her that the truck could roll if it continued to sink further down the rugged hillside.

She shut off the lights, wipers and engine and stared out at the darkness. What were her options? She could sit there until someone came along who could pull her out, but when would that be? The road didn't look as though a car had been over it in years. She had a sudden picture of herself still sitting there behind the wheel of her Bronco, years later—her skeleton gamely clutching the steering wheel, waiting for help from the mountainside.

Selena shuddered. As she became aware of her predicament, she grew increasingly alarmed. She was going to have to do something, but what?

Maybe I can find something to put behind the wheels. She grabbed her jacket, glad she'd had the foresight to bring it, even if it was the middle of June. Mountain nights were notoriously cold. She hadn't counted on the rain to make things worse.

She found a scarf in the glove compartment and wrapped it around her head, then gingerly climbed out of the truck.

Because she was pushing against gravity, the door on her side was even heavier than usual, but she didn't dare slide out the passenger side. In fact, she was afraid to shift her weight at all.

It seemed to take hours before she was out of the truck, standing in the rain and staring with horror at the wheels. They were buried in mud, axle deep.

She sighed. "Well, that does it." Her voice sounded muted in the steady pounding of the rain. Disconsolately she looked around the road and up the hillside. Her searching gaze paused, then she stared toward the summit of the mountain on which she'd been traveling. She saw a flickering light.

Selena blinked, afraid she was imagining things. Wiping the rain from her face, she cupped her hand over her eyes and looked once again. There was definitely a glimmer of light through the trees!

"Wonderful." Her naturally optimistic nature took over once again. Glancing back at the truck, she decided not to bother with her suitcase at the moment. There was time enough to check out the light, then to decide what to do. It didn't look to be far.

Almost half an hour later, Selena had cause to remember the old adage: distances are deceptive in the mountains. For one thing, she wasn't traveling across level ground. There were several gullies to cross and hillsides to struggle up and slide down, and she quickly developed a healthy respect for those intrepid people who enjoy the great outdoors regardless of conditions.

There were times when she thought she'd lost her way, then she would reach the top of a hill and see the light ahead, continuing to beckon to her. When she finally reached the top of a long, grueling incline and discovered a small cabin neatly nestled among the giant boulders and trees, she almost cried with relief.

The light came from a small window near the door of the cabin, and as Selena approached the small structure, the sound of a dog barking ferociously echoed from within. Unless the dog had a megaphone strapped around its neck, it sounded like a very large dog.

At this point, Selena was past being frightened. She was soaking wet, covered in mud and had almost reached the state of total exhaustion. Even if Attila the Hun turned up inside the mysterious cabin, she was still going to beg for shelter.

Only it wasn't Attila the Hun who opened the heavy, wooden door.

The man almost filled the doorway. He was several inches over six feet, with shoulders that seemed to be as wide as the door. Silhouetted as he was she couldn't see his features, but from the way he stood and the quiet confidence he exuded she guessed he was a man in the prime of his life.

The barking was explained. A Great Dane stood by his side watching her intently, as though sizing up his next meal.

While Selena stood there, looking intently at the occupants of the cabin and wondering who they were, they were obviously doing the same.

The man stepped back and motioned her inside, and Selena gratefully entered, glad to be out of the downpour. She had a pretty good idea of what she looked like—something between a drowned cat and a victim of the Flood.

He shut the door behind him, closing out the cold, the damp and the dark night, and enclosing them in the warm, cozy room that was dimly lit by the oil lamp she'd seen in the window and by the dancing flames in a massive fireplace.

Her gaze returned to the man quietly watching her. There was a stillness about him, a gathering of energy that gave her the distinct impression of controlled power. She could feel that he was curious about her, but she sensed that he would not push her for explanations.

The flickering light revealed a face too strong to be handsome, with a strong jawline and a high-bridged nose—a face that spoke of experience and possible hardship, of determination and courage. There was a hint of danger as well.

She stared into the silver-blue eyes, wondering about their secrets, wondering how she knew there *were* secrets. When she could no longer meet that intent, unwavering look, Selena lowered her eyes, then forced herself to look around the room.

She had no clear idea of what she expected, but the neat, one-room cabin was a surprise. It wasn't being used as temporary shelter—the small cabin was a home.

The wide-planked hardwood floor glinted in the soft light and the walls were paneled in knotty pine. Braided rugs dotted the gleaming floor with brilliant color. Bookshelves covered the walls on either side of the stone fireplace. Her gaze fell on a wood-burning cook stove, then moved on to another corner occupied by a king-sized, four-poster bed.

The kerosene lamp sitting on the polished oak table completed the scene, and Selena felt as if she had stepped into the previous century. An open book rested beside the lamp and a large, overstuffed chair stood nearby. He must have been reading.

She finally returned her gaze to the man watching her. An amused glint in his eyes made her realize what she must look like, standing there, dripping on the floor.

Even the dog became bored with its inspection; it ambled over to the fireplace and folded itself into the size of a small camel before the fire.

The man seemed to be waiting for her to say something, but for the life of her, she couldn't think of a sensible remark. Her most lamentable trait, in her own eyes, was her propensity for facetious remarks whenever she was nervous.

"Grizzly Adams, I presume?" she asked in her own famous, husky drawl.

Laughter sparkled in his silver eyes as they shone in the firelight.

"Close. My name is Adam."

He appeared unsurprised at her late-night visit, as though drop-ins on a stormy night were nothing out of the ordinary.

"Well, I'm afraid I'm not Eve, Adam. My name is Selena Stanford." She wondered if he recognized her.

He didn't. *Well, that certainly puts you in your place, doesn't it? Nothing like a drop or two of humility to build character.*

He tilted his head slightly in acknowledgment. "Wouldn't you like to get out of those dripping clothes?"

Her gaze darted back to his face. He seemed serious enough, but the dancing light in his eyes let her know he appreciated the irony of his suggestion.

She gave a breathless chuckle. "My, but you *are* direct. Most men spend at least a few hours in my company before making such a suggestion."

A slow smile appeared on his face and Selena discovered that the smile changed his rather harsh appearance. He was attractive—very attractive, but this was the last thing she should be thinking about at the moment. She glanced down at the pool of water forming at her feet. He was right. She needed to get out of her wet clothes.

She watched him as he walked over to a cabinet and pulled out a large towel. Then he knelt beside the bed and pulled out a drawer underneath and extracted a pair of jeans and a plaid, flannel shirt.

Turning back to her he said, "I'm afraid I'm not enough of a gentleman to leave the room, but I promise to turn my back while you change."

Selena stared down at herself and knew she had no choice. She was shaking with cold as well as nervousness. Gingerly accepting the clothes, she watched him go over to the stove and place a kettle on top. "I'll make you some coffee. Are you hungry?"

Feeling as though she'd stepped onto a television set without knowing her lines, she nodded, then realized he couldn't see her.

"Uh, yes. I *am* hungry and the coffee sounds marvelous."

She edged over to the fire, making sure she didn't disturb the dog that lay there, its massive head resting on crossed paws. She peeled off her jacket and scarf and began to dry her hair.

"What's your dog's name?"

"Duke."

Duke and Adam. Royalty and the first man surviving together on the mountaintop. She hastily unbuttoned her blouse and grabbed his shirt. Although Selena was tall, the shirt swallowed her, coming almost to her knees. She slid her jeans off, relieved to be out of them. She sat down on the edge of the couch and hastily dried her legs. The heat radiating from the fire began to work its magic on her frozen legs and feet.

Her brain seemed to have quit functioning. Too many emotions and sensations circled around within her, and she felt her system had gone into overload. Selina had no fear of the stranger whose home she'd invaded, and she couldn't understand why.

Perhaps she wasn't afraid because she didn't feel that any of this was taking place. Too much had happened to her in too short a time for her to be able to take it in and evaluate it.

"I'm really sorry about barging in on you like this," she said, as she tried once again to dry her hair. "I must have missed my turn, and by the time I realized it, I couldn't find a place to turn around."

"Where were you going?"

"I was going to camp near the park ranger's station. Do you know where that is?"

He turned around and looked at her in surprise. "You were trying to find the park ranger?"

"Yes."

He started laughing. "You're on the wrong side of the mountain for that. Or didn't you know?"

She stared at him in dismay. "You're kidding."

"No. There's only one road that leads to this side from the park—you must have found it."

"You mean this isn't part of Yosemite?"

"No."

"Oh, that's just great."

"Don't worry about it. When this rains lets up, I'll help you turn your car around. You can always follow the road back down, and in the daylight you probably won't have any trouble finding the right turnoff."

"Except for one minor problem. My Bronco has all four wheels buried in the mud." Her disgust was so eloquent that Adam burst out laughing.

She stared at him, amazed at the change in his face that had been almost stern in repose.

She reluctantly smiled in response.

"So you are truly a captive of the mountain tonight?"

"Unfortunately."

He glanced out the window. "You were lucky to find me. I thought you'd come up from the eastern side."

She shook her head, and her drying hair gracefully fell around her shoulders.

"I'm here through sheer luck, the first I've had in some time." She gazed at the firelight in quiet contemplation.

Adam set a bowl and a steaming cup of coffee on the table. He glanced at the woman by the fire and smiled. She looked like a young girl in the oversized shirt. It looked like a dress on her, the collar buttoned neatly under her chin. Her long, slender legs were very shapely and ended in small ankles and bare feet.

Adam had needed the solitude of the last several months—he had not missed having company of any kind, so he was surprised to recognize the pleasure he felt at having this woman suddenly appear. *You'd better watch yourself. You're vulnerable at the moment and you can't afford to let her guess that.*

"Here's your coffee and some stew left over from my dinner."

Selena looked up from studying the fire and smiled. Her smile was one of the beautiful things about her, and he could feel his body reacting to her. *Careful, old boy.*

"Thank you. You're being very kind."

She stepped off the warm rug and paused, her bare toes touching the polished floor.

He spun around and went back to the drawer under the bed. "I'm sorry. I forgot about your feet. Here's a pair of socks that should help."

He handed a pair of thick socks to her, and Selena sat down at the table and pulled them over her cold feet. They felt heavenly. They were tubular socks so that she was able to pull them high on her legs. They came to her knees, and she felt well covered and warm.

Selena picked up the spoon and tasted the stew. It was delicious. Stopping to take a sip of the coffee, she sighed. "Do you have any idea how good this tastes?"

He smiled, a slow half-smile that did queer things to Selena's stomach. She must be hungrier than she thought. "I have an idea. I've been cold and hungry before, myself."

"Oh?" She waited, hoping he would elaborate, but when he didn't, she decided to probe gently. "How long have you lived up here?"

"Almost a year."

"A year! Why would you want to stay up here for so long?"

"To commune with nature?" he whimsically suggested.

"That's a lot of communing. Wasn't it cold up here during the past winter?"

"That's one word for it. I have a kerosene heater that helped the fireplace. And I'm not totally cut off from civilization. I've got a Jeep that gets me where I want to go."

She remembered that she'd found his place from the wrong side. Maybe it wasn't as isolated as it seemed to her. In fact, she had a strong hunch that the whole area would look entirely different to her in the sunlight. She could only hope the sun would be shining the next day.

"What are you doing coming up here camping?" he asked with interest.

"Do you have time to listen to the unedited version, or would you prefer the encapsulated form?"

"One of the benefits of life as a would-be hermit is that there's time enough for everything."

"Well, to begin with, I'm a television actress."

Adam stiffened slightly. "Oh."

"Yes, although I realize that up here you wouldn't have the opportunity to see me. I work on a super-spy series."

Adam lifted his cup to his mouth and sipped the hot liquid.

"Have you ever read any of Kenneth Clay's Derringer Drake novels?"

Adam could feel his muscles tightening, but his face showed no expression. "Yes."

"After the movie was so successful, the powers that be decided to try it as a television series. The author, whose real name is Clay Kenniwick, is a friend of mine and suggested I might want to audition for the part of Derringer's sexy sidekick.'' She sighed. ''Although I was insulted at the time, I wasn't too proud to at least try for the part.''

He looked at her, puzzled, and she laughed. ''You see, I've always considered myself a serious actress and never thought to stoop to frivolous entertainment.'' She shrugged her shoulders slightly. ''Funny how the need to eat regularly and the desire for a place to live will coax you from lofty ideals.'' She shrugged again. ''Anyway, I auditioned and—''

''The rest is history.''

''Yes. The series went over surprisingly well. We've been filming for three years and now I'm suffering from what Clay calls an acute case of burnout.''

''And it was Clay Kenniwick who sent you up here?''

There was an almost imperceptible change in his tone, but Selena caught it. She looked at him quizzically. ''Do you know Clay?''

After a moment's hesitation, he nodded. ''I've met him.''

''No kidding. Well, it's certainly a small world.''

''Is it?''

''What do you mean?''

"Isn't it asking a lot of coincidence that Clay should send you up here on a vacation?"

She looked around the warm and cozy room. "Well, to be honest, he didn't send me here. I had what I thought were clear instructions to the park ranger's headquarters. Obviously I goofed somewhere."

Adam studied her with detached interest. "I'm surprised Clay was willing to let you go on a vacation without him."

Selena looked at him. "How long has it been since you saw Clay?"

"Several years, why?"

She grinned. "That explains it, then. You aren't aware that Clay's been married for over two years now."

Adam recalled the circumstances in which he and Clay met. They hadn't taken time to compare their marital status, even then. "It doesn't seem to interfere with your, uh, friendship."

She straightened from her relaxed position. "Clay and I never had the sort of relationship you're implying, Adam, and I resent your implication. Or maybe you know nothing of friendships without sexual involvement."

He studied the woman sitting there in his shirt and gave her a very seductive smile.

"Well, let's just say I find it hard to believe that anyone would have a platonic relationship with you. Clay didn't strike me as the type who would settle for that."

"Just how well do you know him?"

"We spent several months together a few years ago."

"Where?"

"Eastern Asia."

"For a hermit, you certainly get around."

"I haven't always been a hermit."

"Why did you decide to move up here?"

"I was, uh, recuperating and needed a place that was peaceful and where I wouldn't be disturbed."

"Well, I'm sorry to have been the one to intrude."

"I don't mind in the slightest. I'm enjoying your company."

"Don't enjoy it too much. As soon as it's daylight, I intend to try to get my truck unstuck and find the park ranger." Afraid she'd been unintentionally rude, she hastily added, "I really do appreciate your giving me shelter for the night, though."

He didn't seem to notice. He appeared to be thinking weighty thoughts, from the rather grim expression on his face. He finally roused himself enough to say, "So Clay sent you up here."

"You don't have to make it sound like some espionage plot, you know. He merely writes that stuff. He doesn't live it."

He smiled at her irritated tone. "To be sure." He stood up, stretching to his full height, his arms almost touching the ceiling.

"I'll get you some bedding. You should be comfortable enough there on the couch for the night."

Selena nodded, still irritated by his innuendos. Morning couldn't come soon enough as far as she was concerned. The guy had been living alone too long—he was downright eccentric.

Hours later, Adam lay awake in his wide, comfortable bed, wondering about the beautiful woman sleeping soundly in front of the fire. She could very well be exactly who she said she was. It made sense that she wouldn't use a cover that could be so easily disproved by checking a television series.

But what was her real purpose in coming up here—alone? Was Clay behind it? Could it be possible Clay had found out he was up here? Adam thought he had covered his tracks better than that.

The man Clay knew was supposedly missing and presumed dead. Only one man, his former boss, knew that he had managed to escape—barely—with his life. With his help, Adam had become another person with a whole new background. He had done his best to put his past behind him and thought he had succeeded.

Could it be a coincidence? Adam turned over on his stomach and buried his head in his pillow. He wished to hell he believed in coincidences!

Chapter Two

Selena slowly awoke to the sound of heavy breathing close to her ear. Suddenly, she remembered where she was. She had spent the night in a stranger's cabin—alone with him. Her eyes blinked open in alarm. Duke stood next to the couch, nuzzling her, and she allowed herself a deep sigh of relief.

Bright sunlight danced around the room in morning splendor. *At least one of my wishes came true,* she decided with a warm feeling. *The weather is cooperating a little better today.*

She sat up, glancing across the room at the bed, but it was empty. In fact, she and Duke were the sole occupants of the place. Her clothes were dry from having hung in front of the fire all night, and Selena gratefully slipped them back on. Although the shirt she'd borrowed had made a warm nightgown for her, she felt more comfortable now that her wearing apparel was back to normal.

She managed to get the tangles out of her hair with the small brush she carried in her purse, then she decided to search for the hygienic facilities. They were obviously not in the house, and Selena walked over to the door and opened it.

The view was spellbinding. Majestic mountain peaks seemed to surround the area. The sun picked out the colors in the trees and bushes, emphasizing the green of the early summer. But it was the sounds—the soft chirping of the sparrows, the steady knocking of the woodpeckers, and the scolding of the squirrels—that disarmed her. The sounds of summer in the quiet of the mountains flowed over her, making the tensions and stresses of her life melt away.

Clay had been right to suggest a vacation in the mountains.

But other matters loomed on her list of priorities. Fortunately, Selena spotted a path leading behind the cabin and optimistically followed it. She found a small outhouse sheltered under the trees.

Outdoor life had certain drawbacks, she decided on her way back to the cabin, but on the whole, she knew she'd enjoy the next few weeks.

Selena pushed open the door to the cabin, then paused, nonplussed. Standing near the bed and directly in her view was Adam. He faced away from the door as he reached for a shirt, and the bright, morning sunlight gave his dark tan a rosy hue. Selena looked intently at his muscular back, particularly at the scar that seemed to glow at his waist as though a highlighter had placed emphasis on the taut muscles there. A long, thin scar creasing his shoulder blade and several indentations across his back gave proof of further damage done in the past.

He spun around at the sound of the door. "Good morning," he said casually, slipping his arms through the sleeves of his shirt.

Seldom was Selena at a loss for words, but her mind seemed to have blanked out. She had watched makeup men strive for the effect she'd just seen on Adam's back. They had been amazingly successful, because now Selena recognized that these were scars from more than one bullet wound.

Why would this man have been shot?

He smiled, the half smile that was becoming familiar to her—a slight lifting of the corner of his mouth. ''I made some coffee. Help yourself.''

She seemed to be frozen to the door. Why had she felt so relaxed around him last night? Perhaps because she'd been too tired to care. But this morning all of her fears of unknown assailants came back to haunt her.

She could feel perspiration on her forehead and moisture on her palms as they pressed against the wooden door. She was much closer to the door than he and drew strength from this rather reassuring knowledge.

He glanced up from stuffing his shirttail into the waist of his Levi's. ''Is something wrong?''

She shook her head.

''You don't really need to look as though I intend to hack your body into little pieces, you know. I had all the opportunity I needed last night but decided it would take too much energy.''

She jumped slightly at his comment. Where were all of her acting abilities now, when she needed them? Her attempt at a laugh was a miserable failure. She sounded as nervous as she felt—and no doubt looked.

Your overactive imagination is doing it again, Selena, she told herself, *and you're making a complete fool of yourself.*

She forced herself to walk over to the stove, pick up the coffee pot and pour herself a cup, but she kept him in her side vision all the while. "I really do thank you for letting me stay here last night," she managed to say in a light voice. "I think I'll get back to the truck and see about getting it unstuck." She looked over at him and smiled.

He nodded, wondering what had caused her to become so jumpy all of a sudden. Not that he cared, but he was curious. "Would you like me to come along and help?"

She studied him for a moment. There was really nothing to be afraid of. He looked at her directly, his eyes calmly meeting hers. He didn't seem to have anything to hide. There could be several legitimate reasons to have the scars on his back. He could have been in the war, for instance. She found the thought reassuring.

"If you don't mind, I would appreciate your help," she finally answered.

"Then I suggest we eat something first. I don't like to work on an empty stomach."

The hike down to the road was much more pleasant in the morning light than it had been the night before. The porous ground had absorbed much of the moisture, and Selena no longer felt threatened by man, beast or nature. However, the roadway still seemed an interminable distance away.

"You hiked from down here last night?" Obviously Adam was just as surprised at the distance.

"Yes."

"No wonder you were exhausted when you found me."

"I'm beginning to realize how lucky I was to find anyone. You don't have many neighbors, do you?"

He grinned. "None that I know of."

When they finally reached the road, Selena wasn't surprised that the truck wasn't in sight. But she couldn't decide which way to go to look for it.

"Do you suppose we should split up, then yell when we spot it?" she suggested.

Adam looked around the quiet area, the large trees casting mottled shade along the path. "I suppose that would be the most sensible thing to do." He glanced at her. "Try not to get lost."

"Believe me, I don't intend to take any chances."

Adam disappeared around the curve of the road and Selena started uphill once more. She hadn't gone very far when she heard Adam's call. "That figures," she murmured under her breath. If she'd gone that way, he would have found the car up here somewhere.

Selena trotted down the roadway until she saw Adam. He was standing in the middle of the road, waiting for her with a grim expression on his face. She didn't see the Bronco.

"What's wrong?" she asked, a little out of breath.

"That's what I want you to tell me." He studied her suspiciously.

She looked up and down the road. Nothing looked familiar. This was another curve in a road full of them. "The truck must be down the road further."

"Or there never was one."

She stared at him, wondering if there was something mentally wrong with him as well. "Of course there was. I told you it was buried to the axles last night."

He waved to the side of the road where Selena noticed for the first time the ground was rutted. "Or you had someone drop you off, so I would think you were stranded."

"But I'm not stranded. I just got the truck stuck."

"Then why isn't the truck here now?"

"How should I know?"

"But this is where you left it last night, isn't it?"

She stared around in confusion. "I really have no idea. There were no landmarks—it was dark and raining hard. Why don't we keep looking?"

"Because I don't intend to waste any more time on whatever little game you're playing." He pointed to the opposite side of the road from where they were looking. "That *is* your suitcase, isn't it? That you so conveniently left to pick up later?"

Selena spun around and looked to where he was pointing. Her suitcase was sitting by the side of the road—the same suitcase she had left locked up in the Bronco last night.

Or had she locked it? Hastily she dug in her purse, then in her pockets. No keys. She tried to remember if she had taken them out of the ignition.

She remembered inching out of the truck, pushing against the door to get out and finally managing to wriggle through the narrow opening. She did not remember taking the keys with her.

"My truck's been stolen!"

"Nice try. I wondered how long it would take you to try that one. Now why don't you admit it? You and your friends decided to see how I'd react if you showed up on my doorstep last night, cold and tired. Well, now you know. I hope it was worth all of your efforts." He turned around and started back up the hillside.

"Wait a minute. You've got it all wrong. I've been telling you the truth. I left the truck here last night. It must have been here, because those tracks show where I skidded off the road. I must have forgotten the keys and somebody came along, got the truck unstuck and stole it."

"You actually expect me to believe that story?"

"Well, since it's the truth, yes, I do. Besides, it makes a lot more sense than your theory. Why would I go to all that trouble just to meet you?"

"You tell me."

"Look, Adam, I don't know who you are, nor do I care. You may be some famous personality hiding away up here. If you are, I promise not to tell a soul. I'm sorry if your ego is bruised because I didn't recognize you. But I never knew you existed until you answered your door last night."

They stood on either side of the road, glaring at each other. Adam reminded himself that she was a self-acknowledged actress, and from that recent performance he had to admit she was a good one. Her bewilderment and pathos were very well done.

"What do you want from me?" he asked quietly.

"Nothing! All I want is to find my truck and find the park ranger." She looked at him wistfully. "You don't by any chance have a phone, do you?"

He continued to stare at her without expression.

"I didn't really think so." She surveyed the area with dismay. "Do you have any transportation that would get me back to civilization?"

"My Jeep would take you down to the eastern side of the mountain." He eyed her for a moment. "I suppose I could take you to the closest town."

She smiled in relief. "That would be fine. I just need to get to a phone and report the Bronco stolen."

"You still insist you don't know how it disappeared?"

"Yes, I do. Why in the world would you think otherwise?"

"Lack of trust, perhaps?" he asked sarcastically.

"How about a good case of paranoia?"

They started back toward the cabin in strained silence, Selena carrying her heavy case. Halfway back, Adam reached over and took the case, much to Selena's grateful relief.

By the time they reached the cabin, Selena was ashamed of her outburst. He'd been kind to her last night—and this morning. There was no reason for her to take out her frustrations on him.

"Thank you for helping me with my suitcase."

"You're welcome." He glanced at the horizon, avoiding her eyes, then looked down at her again. "Are you ready to go?"

"Yes."

He walked around the cabin. "The Jeep is parked down the hill this way." They hiked for several hundred yards through the trees until they came to a clearing. Selena smiled when she saw the dilapidated Jeep. The poor thing looked as though it should have been put out to pasture several years ago.

Adam began to curse under his breath and she looked at him in surprise. He walked over to the right front tire and knelt down. Selena realized the tire was flat.

"What happened?"

He strode around the Jeep, checking each tire. All four of them were flat. "Your friends were thorough," he said in a tight voice. "They slashed all of them, including the spare."

"Your tires are slashed?" Then she realized what else he'd said. "*My* friends. What are you accusing me of now?"

"You're really good, you know that? Shocked surprise and wounded indignation. No wonder you've made it as an actress."

"Damn you. I haven't the faintest idea what is going on around here, nor why you insist I do!"

"Because you turned up—and now my tires are slashed."

Selena stomped over to Adam. "Will you stop blaming me for my truck being missing and your tires being slashed? I have no more idea why this has happened than you do. As far as that goes, you could have some powerful enemies yourself.''

She slumped down on a large rock and looked blankly at the disabled vehicle. Now what was she going to do? Never had she wanted to get away from anyone so much in her life—and never had she been so stranded!

Adam watched her warily, then he began to study the ground around the Jeep. Whoever had done it was a professional. Although he found one or two slight indentations, there was nothing so clear as a footprint, and he couldn't tell if more than one person had been there.

He followed the trail down the hill for about a quarter of a mile and came across tire tracks. Whoever had decided to immobilize them had gone, but for how long?

And where did Selena fit into all of this?

''We might as well go back to the cabin and decide how you're going to get out of here,'' he said.

''I have no intention of returning to that cabin.''

''Suit yourself. You now know two roads you can follow out of here. Have fun walking. It should be good exercise for you.''

Adam disappeared along the path on which they had come, leaving Selena sitting there, dismally staring down the road.

"I've been working on that damned series too long. My mind immediately runs to espionage and agents. But I'd love to know what's happening here and why my truck was stolen." *And who Adam really is.*

Did she want to hike out of there? Not particularly, but she probably didn't have much choice. She stood up and lifted her suitcase. When she had packed it, she hadn't given a thought to having to carry it for any distance. Perhaps she'd leave it with Adam and come back for it later. Surely he wouldn't mind keeping it for her.

With new determination and resolve, Selena started up the hill toward the cabin, carrying the suitcase. She heard Duke barking before she reached the cabin. At least he made a good watchdog.

With a suddenness she could scarcely believe, someone grabbed her from behind, and an arm snaked around her throat. What her assailant didn't know was that one of Selena's skills, sharpened during the series, was the ability to scream instantly, a sharp, ear-piercing sound that she used every time a dead body turned up in the script for her to find.

Her scream was one of her best efforts—her director would have been pleased.

Not so her would-be captor. Her scream was

abruptly cut off by a hand that was clapped over her nose and mouth, a hand holding a small piece of cloth soaked in chloroform.

Adam heard the scream. He had just returned to the cabin with an armful of wood. Instinct made him grab his pistol and run outside.

When he rounded the corner of the cabin, he froze. Two men were carrying Selena—a seemingly lifeless Selena—away from the cabin.

Adam took careful aim and fired the pistol, then he started toward them. He watched with growing horror as the men dropped her and ran off, one of them holding his arm.

His heart pounding, Adam raced to her side. "Selena!" He quickly felt for her pulse, and saw that she was breathing. Then he sighed with relief. She was unconscious but otherwise seemed to be unhurt. His hands were shaking, not a good sign. He had always been known for his steady nerves.

After double checking to be sure she wasn't injured, Adam carefully gathered her into his arms. Holding her close to him, he could smell the distinctive, sweet odor of the anesthetic.

"What have you done to get them chasing after you?" he muttered. Determined to get some answers, he strode toward the cabin.

Chapter Three

Selena's head felt as though it had been used as an oversized baseball for batting practice. She moaned slightly, reluctantly opening her eyes.

A pair of silver-blue eyes stared intently at her from a few inches away. They were surrounded by thick, black lashes that made them appear even lighter. She shut her eyes, then reopened them, trying to focus on the eyes watching her.

She glanced around and discovered she was lying on Adam's four-poster bed. His mammoth dog lay on a rug nearby, watching her with interest. Selena carefully eased her hand behind her head and discovered a large bump.

"Why did you grab me?" she asked plaintively.

"*I* didn't. Two men did their best to carry you off."

She stared at him in suspicion. "You didn't want me here."

He nodded his head in agreement. "True, but I hadn't reached the point where I felt the need to chloroform you and drag you away somewhere."

She thought about that for a moment. "Who did?"

"A good question. A very good question, I might add. They must have tried to get into the cabin until Duke discouraged them."

"I heard barking but thought it was at me."

"When I saw them, they dropped you and ran." He saw no need to mention the shot he'd fired. Continuing to study her, he asked with a smile, "How do you manage to look so enticing when you're unconscious?"

"You know, I'm not at all sure I understand your sense of humor. Maybe you've lived alone too long."

In a more serious tone, he said, "I suppose it's too much to hope that you might have recognized them."

"No. I thought it was you."

"Please believe me when I tell you I had nothing to do with it."

"Okay, if you'll believe I've had nothing to do with anything that has happened since I got my truck stuck in the mud."

They glared at each other beligerently. Finally, Adam gave a short nod. "All right. It's gone beyond a practical joke, even if Clay were so inclined. So where does that leave us?"

"Darned if I know. I don't understand any of this."

Adam sighed in disgust. "That makes two of us."

Selena absently noted that Adam was sitting next to her on the bed, leaning across her and, propped up by his arm, pressed close to her side. He was studying her.

"Why are you looking at me like that?" she finally asked.

"Like what?"

"Like I'm some strange species found only under a microscope."

"Actually I was thinking about what a beautiful woman you are."

She closed her eyes for a moment. "Why is it I don't believe my looks have anything to do with why you're staring at me."

"They don't?"

"No. You're wondering why my truck was stolen, your tires slashed, and why I was almost carried off."

"I see. Do you participate in some sort of mind-reading act when you're not filming your television series?"

Selena wished he would move. He was entirely too close. She could smell the subtle scent of after-shave, a woodsy odor that seemed to blend in with their surroundings. "No, I don't. It doesn't take much brain power to know you're more concerned over what's been happening than you are over me."

"Not necessarily." Adam leaned even further, his face coming closer. She looked up at him, startled. There was a definite gleam in his eyes—one she hadn't seen before. He appeared much closer than he had been earlier. What did he think he was doing?

His lips reached hers and there was no longer any doubt in Selena's mind what he was doing. He was doing a damn good job of kissing her. His mouth caressed hers with an expertise that had not been learned living as a hermit on a mountainside. The jolt of electricity that shot through her at his touch generated enough power to light up the entire cabin as well as several appliances.

Selena had been the recipient of any number of kisses during her twenty-five years—stage kisses, television kisses, fumbling, moist, heavy-breathing kisses that had left her cold.

Adam's kiss did not fit into any of those categories. For one thing, there was nothing tentative about it—nor groping. His hands remained on either side of her body, so she couldn't explain why her hands slid up his chest and around his neck, inquisitively exploring the thick, sable-brown hair that flowed like silk through her fingers.

Her lips parted and he shifted slightly, slanting his mouth over hers in a possessiveness that caused a quivering sensation deep in the pit of her stomach. His tongue lightly explored the surface of her lips, brushing against them until they opened in invitation. He settled closer to her, his tongue teasing hers in a delicate duel. Selena found herself responding to him, her headache forgotten.

When he eventually pulled away from her, a quizzical smile on his face, Selena realized she'd lost all track of time, of where she was, with whom, and why.

They gazed at each other in silence, each

her into a boneless mass of simmering heat; the next minute he was making all sorts of innuendos that infuriated her. Now he was mocking her and she yearned to be able to plant her fist in his face.

Counting very slowly and with intense concentration, Selena managed not to tell Adam exactly what she thought of him, his behavior and his mountain country. "Do you have a better suggestion?" she finally managed to ask in a quiet voice.

He faced her, leaning against the window's edge and crossing his arms over his broad chest. "As a matter of fact, I do. Why don't you stay up here and help me find out what's going on?"

"Why in the world would I want to do that?"

"You don't care that you were almost abducted today? And what about your stolen truck?"

"Of course I care. Why do you think I'm so anxious to report it?"

"But it hasn't yet occurred to you that this is more than a casual theft, has it? You're so used to life in the big city that car theft has become a way of life for you."

He was right. She hadn't given much

thought to why her truck was missing. Anyone stupid enough to leave keys in a vehicle could automatically assume it would be taken. But on a deserted mountainside during a storm?

"Who would take it?"

"Ahhhhh. A very good question. Could it be the same person or persons who slashed my tires and grabbed you? In other words, is there some reason you and I are not supposed to leave the mountain at the moment?"

Selena thought about his questions. Not many people knew where she had planned to go. Clay and Carolyn had helped her plan the trip. Carolyn had gone shopping with her to find suitable clothes, and Clay had supervised her camping equipment.

"My camping equipment!"

"What are you talking about?"

"I had a sleeping bag, small tent, cook stove and a battery-operated lamp in that Bronco. They took my suitcase out of the truck. Why didn't they leave my camping equipment?"

"Good question. Maybe they're going to be using it?" His eyes traveled over her in an encompassing sweep that made Selena feel that he could accurately describe her clothes size in the most intimate detail. "They probably couldn't wear your clothes."

Selena sank down into the comfortably stuffed recliner and wearily leaned her had back against the headrest. Her head still felt woolly and this conversation wasn't helping any. "How could I help you find out what's going on?"

"That depends. It may be that it's just coincidence that you and I are left stranded up here—a case of being in the wrong place at the wrong time. But from the looks of it, someone wants you specifically." He straightened up from his lounging position and walked over to the coffee pot. Placing it on the stove, he fed some small pieces of wood into the grate then turned to look at her.

"Why don't you tell me more about yourself, Selena? Perhaps you know something you aren't aware of knowing that someone feels is a threat to them."

"That's crazy, Adam. You know something? You've been up here on your own too long." She waved a hand at the bookshelves full to overflowing. "You've been reading too many adventure books." She shook her head. "And I thought *I* had too much imagination." She watched him as he poured them each a cup of coffee. Setting up the cups on the table by her chair, he pulled out the other chair from the table and sat down across from her.

"When did you leave your home yesterday?"

"About two o'clock."

"Were you followed?"

"Of course not!"

"Why are you so adamant?"

"Because there's no reason for anyone to follow me."

"Only to steal your car."

"Yes. No. I don't know. I'm sure nobody was following me because I ended up having to backtrack several miles when I took the wrong turn and came across a tractor-trailer that was obviously lost."

"Why do you say that?"

"Well, it had all kinds of antennas and satellite dishes on it, sitting out in the middle of nowhere. At least I had room to turn around and go back the way I'd come in."

"Do you know what sort of antennas it had?"

"No. All I know is that it was a dead end and I realized I'd made a wrong turn. So I had to drive back several miles. I would have seen a car if I'd been followed."

Adam leaned closer to her, his eyes gleaming silver in the darkening room. "Please try to describe what you saw on that truck. It may be very important."

Selena glanced out the window. Clouds were rolling in and covering the sun. She wouldn't be at all surprised if it started raining. "I don't know what it was. I didn't look at it all that closely."

"Did you see anyone?"

"No, but then I didn't look. When I realized the road stopped there, I knew I was in the wrong place so I turned around and left."

"Did you see any cars?"

"There may have been."

"Think! You may have stumbled onto something you had no business seeing."

"What do you mean?"

"I'm not sure. I'm trying to remember what I read recently about some signals being jammed on some of our communications satellites." He studied his cup for several minutes while Selena studied him.

She wondered how old he was. He looked to be in his early forties until he smiled. When he smiled, ten years disappeared. It was too bad he didn't smile more often. He had a beautifully shaped mouth—and she suddenly remembered how his lips felt against hers.

Adam finally spoke. "The government is testing a new communcations satellite. It's supposed to be sensitive enough to pick up and transmit signals never before received. It's supposed to warn us of any potential threat that might be aimed toward us."

"Such as?"

"Missiles aimed at the west coast from foreign submarines."

She stood up. "All right. That does it. I don't want to hear any more." She wandered over to the window and watched as the rain began to pour from the sky. "Isn't it enough that I make my living portraying the helpful sidekick of Derringer Drake without spending my vacation trying to sift for clues regarding espionage, foreign submarines and threats of missiles, satellites and secret tracking stations?"

"How did you intend to spend your vacation?"

She glanced over her shoulder. "From the looks of things, watching rain." She looked back out the window.

What if Adam were right? What if his armchair sleuthing all winter had caused him to pick up on something that was really happening here on the mountain?

What was she supposed to do about it? All she wanted was to have some peace and quiet, maybe to work on her tan; at most, to return to Los Angeles with a better understanding of where her career was heading and where she wanted it to go. She didn't care about what the government was doing, nor about who was spying on whom.

She turned around and resolutely faced her reluctant host. "I don't think I'm going to be going anywhere until the rain lets up. But as soon as it does, I'm going to start hiking out of here. Sooner or later I'll find a ride or a telephone or something." She smiled. "It's not that I don't appreciate your hospitality, but this was not what I had in mind for a vacation."

Why did it bother him to hear her planning to leave? He had never laid eyes on her before last night. She meant nothing to him. *Oh, yeah?* a small voice asked.

So he was more lonesome than he realized. It was good to talk to someone other than Duke, whose level of conversation left something to be desired.

It was nothing to do with the fact she's gor-

geous, intelligent, and has a smile that would melt steel at twenty paces.

Go to hell, he told the small voice venomously.

The room was quiet as the tension between the two of them continued to build. Lightning made the sky glow and Selena groaned. Another storm—just what she needed. There was no way she was going to be able to get out of there tonight.

"Well, since you are so graciously accepting my hospitality for another evening, I'd better do something about feeding us."

Adam began to pull items from his cupboards and Selena resolutely went over to the fireplace. "Would you like me to start a fire?" she finally asked.

He grinned. "If you know how."

She glared at him. "Do I really look that helpless?"

"No comment."

Selena raked through the coals, found some warm ones and began to add kindling. "No comment," she muttered under her breath. "That's a comment in itself." She sat back on her heels and admired the way her fire took hold.

Standing, she said, "Where could I wash

up?'' Without looking around, Adam grabbed a pump handle and began to pump it industriously until water gushed out. ''If you want me to warm it for you, I can.''

Selena had never seen a water pump like that before. He really was living a primitive existence up here. She wondered why.

She finally got up the nerve to question him after dinner. He hadn't turned the lamp on, and they sat in front of the cheery fire, its heat warming the room. Adam had poured them brandy and they sipped on it while they sat on the couch in front of the fire, watching the flames.

''What did you do before you decided to become a hermit?''

A long pause followed her question and she wondered if he were going to ignore it. ''I was in the import-export business for several years,'' he finally answered, ''but grew tired of the constant travel.''

''Were you ever in the armed services?''

''The Navy. Why do you ask?''

''No reason. I was just curious.'' About the scars on his back, among other things. Where had he gotten them?

She was distracted from her thoughts by Duke's strange behavior. Adam had let him out earlier in the evening. When he returned inside, he had allowed Adam to wipe him dry, then he settled in front of the fire. Now he paced restlessly around the room.

"What's the matter with Duke?"

Adam glanced around and watched him for a moment. "He senses something outside. You have to remember we're out here with nature. There's no telling what's prowling around."

He had no sooner finished speaking when Duke made a lunge at the door, barking ferociously. Adam suddenly grabbed her, luckily right after she had placed her snifter on the table, and rolled to the floor with her, so that when they landed he completely covered her.

"What are you—"

"Quiet. There's somebody outside."

"Or some animal."

"No," he whispered. "Duke doesn't bark like that at an animal."

They lay there motionless, listening. Selena was soon distracted by Adam's close proximity. Although he was on top of her, he was supporting most of his weight so that she could breathe. But they were carefully aligned so that he touched her everywhere, from her chin to her toes.

She could feel the hard surface of his chest pressing against hers, hear his harsh breathing near her ear, and slowly recognized the effect she was having on him. "Would you kindly explain to me the necessity of sprawling on top of me?" she demanded in a fierce whisper. "I can't breathe," she added for good measure. Her lack of breath had little to do with his weight. It had more to do with the sensations she was experiencing. She knew he was experiencing similar ones.

Meanwhile Duke was going through all the antics of a wild dog fighting to get out of captivity.

Adam slid to the side and, keeping below the windows crawled over to the darkest part of the room and peered out the window.

"Who would be dumb enough to be out in this kind of weather?" she asked in a low tone.

"The same people who were out in it last night. They're still after something—or somebody." He glanced around at her and noticed that her eyes seemed to have grown larger in the last few minutes. "Don't worry. I won't let them harm you."

Why didn't she feel more reassured? If

someone was after her, how was *she* going to stop them?

Duke gradually settled down, looking pleased with himself. Perhaps he should be, Selena thought. His barking may have scared whoever it was away.

Adam stood up and offered his hand to Selena. She pulled herself up and sat down again on the couch. "I want you to sleep in the bed tonight," he stated. "It's farther from the door. If anyone decides to come visiting, I'll be waiting for them right here."

"Would you quit being so damn dramatic, Adam? Maybe this is how you entertain yourself up here all by yourself, but frankly, I don't appreciate it. You're scaring the hell out of me."

"Sorry." He sat down beside her, kissing her mouth lightly. Pulling back slightly, he looked into her eyes. Whatever he saw made him smile. Adam pulled her into his arms and kissed her again. His hands slid along her back in a gentle motion and Selena relaxed in his arms. She couldn't get over the strange effect he had on her.

This has got to stop, she reminded herself. Pushing against his chest, Selena said, "Look,

Adam, I appreciate your hospitality, but I don't intend to repay you in this manner.''

He laughed. He actually laughed. She knew she didn't care for his sense of humor. Not at all.

She got up from the couch. "I don't want to take your bed. I'm sure I'll be perfectly safe here on the couch. After all, I'll have Duke to protect me."

Adam stood up and bent over the fire, rearranging the existing logs and placing new ones on it. "Do whatever you want." He walked over to his bed and knelt. Pulling the drawer out, he palmed something, then stood up.

"I don't know what's going on, but I'm not going to let you go out there alone to use the facility."

He said it as though he expected an argument, but he certainly wasn't going to get one from her. His jumpiness was infectious and his presence would be most welcome.

Selena picked up her coat and started for the door.

"Wait a minute."

She glanced back over her shoulder at him.

"Why don't you wait here a moment, while Duke and I go out first?"

"Fine with me. Just whistle when you want me."

The sudden smile on his face made her wish she could retract that last statement, but she refused to give him the satisfaction of knowing she was flustered.

"Let's go, Duke."

Selena watched them leave the cabin, Duke bounding out of the door and disappearing. She couldn't help but feel a little sorry for the unsuspecting soul who might be there if Duke got hold of him. Several minutes later, Adam opened the door. "Whoever was out here is gone, but he left enough prints to know he was here."

Selena shivered. She thrust her arms through her coat sleeves and followed him out the door. At least it had quit raining and the sky was beginning to clear. There was no moon, but the stars looked close enough to touch.

Adam directed the beam of the flashlight in front of them, and they walked to the small outbuilding in silence. He opened the door and made sure there was no one inside to surprise her, then stepped back with a polite motion of his hand.

Without saying a word, Selena stepped inside and closed the door, effectively cutting off the light. Great. Just what she needed. She didn't waste much time inside and was relieved to see Adam waiting several feet away when she stepped out.

They returned to the cabin in silence.

"Is the solitude of the mountains getting to you, or don't you have anything to say?" he asked quietly as they stepped back into the cabin. Duke followed them in and returned to his rug in front of the fireplace.

"I don't like any of this," she finally admitted.

"Neither do I."

"I just wish we had a phone up here."

"As a matter of fact, that thought has crossed my mind more than once during the past few hours."

She glanced around the room uncertainly. "Where could I change my clothes?"

"You'll be more comfortable by the fire." He walked over to the other end of the room and checked the window.

At least I have my own clothes, she thought as she flipped open the lid of her suitcase and reached for her gown. There wasn't much to it, but it was the most comfortable thing she had. She hated pajamas. After slipping on the shortie nightgown, she pulled her heavy robe over her shoulders and quickly knotted the belt.

Adam had brought over some blankets and a pillow, the same bedding she had used the night before, and she made herself a warm bed on the couch.

She stretched out on the couch with a sigh. "This is great, Adam. Thank you."

"Any time. I'll talk to you in the morning."

He lay in bed trying to decide what to do about their unwanted visitors. It wasn't his way to sit and wait for something to happen. If it weren't for Selena, he'd be outside tracking whoever was out there. Whoever it was had gotten careless, or the rain had made it too difficult not to leave prints.

He would come up with a plan by morning. He needed to get her out of there and back on track with her vacation plans. Moreover, he needed no reminders of what it was like to have a woman around. Unfortunately, the reminder was already there and he recognized the attraction he felt for her—just as he recognized he had no intention of pursuing the attraction.

Adam had lived his life as a loner and he preferred it that way. He just wished the little voice in his head would quit arguing the point.

Chapter Four

Selena was caught up in her dream, at least she sincerely hoped it was a dream. She was being held captive and she was waiting for Derringer—or was it Adam—to rescue her.

A hand reached out and touched her lightly on the shoulder. She screamed.

Duke started barking and Adam's curses joined the general confusion. "Dammit, Selena, you don't have to act like I'm attacking you!"

Confused, Selena sat up and looked around the room. A faint light filtered through the windows. "What's wrong?"

Duke decided there was nothing he needed to do at the moment, so he stretched out once again with a sigh. Adam ran his hand through his already rumpled hair. "Nothing's wrong. I just wanted to wake you up."

"You certainly did that. Now that I'm awake, what do you want?"

"I want you to show me where you found that truck with electronic equipment."

"Certainly. I'll jump on my trusty steed and we'll be there in no time."

Adam sat down on the edge of the couch, entirely too close to Selena as far as she was concerned.

"It won't be that easy, I'm afraid. We'll have to walk."

She stared at him in surprise. "You're serious about this, aren't you?"

"Yes. We've got to find out what's going on and why you were followed up here."

"It's several miles from here, you know."

"I'm not surprised, but you planned to hike out of here anyway."

She yawned. "So I did, but I'd planned on starting out at a decent hour." She glanced out the window. "This *is* my vacation, you know."

He grinned. "I know and I'm sorry, but I have a feeling we're going to need all the daylight we can get before today's over. Why don't you get dressed while I make break-fast.''

Why not? I'm awake now, she thought waspishly. ''Good idea. I wonder why I didn't think of it?'' She smiled at him, a smile so sweet he doubted its sincerity. With good reason.

He leaned toward her, clearly intending to kiss her. She stopped him by placing her hand on his chest. ''Would you cut that out?''

''Why?''

''Why? Why? Because we don't know each other, that's why. Because we're caught up in crazy circumstances or we wouldn't even be staying together, that's why. Because—''

''All right, I get your message.'' He stood up and stretched, his arms high above his head and she gazed at the muscles that rippled under the snug, knit shirt. He looked down at her, buried in her blankets. ''How did you sleep?''

''Reasonably well, although either you or Duke snore.''

''I'm afraid I can't take credit for that. I forgot to warn you about him.'' They both glanced at Duke who watched them with friendly interest, aware that his name had been mentioned in their conversation.

"I've seen Shetland ponies smaller than he is," Selena offered.

"I know, but when I saw him as a puppy I knew we would become great friends. And we have."

"Are you going to take him with us on our hiking jaunt?"

"No. But he'll be all right up here by himself. I'll leave enough food and water."

"And when he needs to go out?"

"He has a way in and out that we built for emergencies."

"I see. Well—" She eyed him thoughtfully.

"What's the matter?"

"I'm waiting for you to depart to the kitchen—" she waved her hand in the general direction of that corner of the cabin "—so I can get up."

"You're very modest, aren't you?"

"Not particularly, but I don't intend to provide your early morning entertainment, either."

Adam turned around and strolled to the stove. "Are you ready for coffee?"

"You bet." She eased out of the covers, feeling the early morning chill against her legs. Quickly digging through her clothes, she found jeans and a warm sweater. The soft blue of the top matched the color of her eyes and made a nice contrast to her long, blond hair. After vigorously brushing it, she pulled her hair high on top of her head, pinning it securely.

Adam handed her a cup of coffee. Gratefully she accepted it and took a sip. He really wasn't all that bad, she supposed. A mite eccentric, but then, everyone has his or her little hang-ups. Hers was that she'd like to find something a little more serious to act in, while the Derringer Drake series had made her a household name. *Why aren't we ever satisfied with what we have?* she wondered. Still, it would be much more rewarding to be remembered for her acting abilities rather than her plunging necklines.

Adam watched her while she ate the plate of food he'd placed in front of her. He was surprised at how quiet she was. Most women he'd known felt uncomfortable with silence and attempted to fill it with inane chatter. Not Selena. He wondered what she was thinking with such a serious expression on her face. He also wondered why he cared.

"I'd like to make a suggestion." Adam finally broke the silence.

"Fire away."

"You might want to take a change of clothing—something dark, in case we don't make it back before dark."

She studied him for a moment. He wore a black knit shirt and black corduroy pants. "All right." As soon as she finished eating, she got up and dug through her belongings once more.

When they were ready to go, Adam walked over to Duke and knelt down beside him, murmuring something. Duke watched him alertly, as though he understood every word, then placed his chin on his paws with a sigh.

"Let's go." Adam opened the door and stepped outside.

The sun was just peeking over the eastern mountain ridge and Selena paused, drinking in the beauty of the early morning. Although she had intended to spend her time alone, she had to admit she didn't mind Adam's presence. There was something about him that made her feel he could be trusted and that he was capable of taking care of both of them. She hoped her instincts were sound. Otherwise, she could find herself in trouble.

Adam glanced around the clearing with an alertness that caused a twinge of uneasiness within her. She shrugged the feeling away. With a measured gait, Selena attempted to match her steps to Adam's. When they reached the shelter of trees, he paused.

"I don't like the feel of this."

"Whatever are you talking about?"

Before he could respond a low voice spoke directly behind them. "Turn around slowly, if you will."

Adam followed the order precisely—each movement carefully calibrated. Selena swung around with a start—and gasped.

The man standing behind them held a snub-nosed pistol in his right hand. His navy-blue windbreaker and denim jeans caused him to blend into the shadows of the trees.

Adam's voice sounded calm and very reasonable to Selena. "What do you want?"

"We're making a security check of the area. This young woman was seen in a restricted area recently and needs to be detained until positive identification can be made." The man's voice was low but clear.

Selena relaxed slightly. At least he wasn't some gangster.

"Who are you?" Adam asked.

"We're with the Secret Service."

Selena sighed with disgust. "Then why all this sneaking around? Why didn't you just knock on the door last night."

The man looked startled. "Last night?"

"Yes. And why did you slash the tires, steal the truck and try to carry me off yesterday?"

The stranger's face seemed to freeze into an impassive mask. "I know nothing about that."

Adam shifted slightly. "Why are you holding a gun on us?"

The man glanced down at his hand as though surprised to see the pistol. "You can't be too careful these days." He looked past them and Selena glanced around, surprised to see two men standing among the trees, watching them. He glanced back at Selena. "If you'll just come along with us, miss, we'll get the matter cleared in no time."

His suggestion sounded reasonable to Selena, and she turned to Adam to thank him for his offer of help.

"I'm going with you." He gave Selena a mocking smile. "You see, I've invested too much in her already to let something happen to her now." He met the other man's steady gaze. "She's my wife."

Selena watched the scene before her, realizing with a shock that she was waiting for the director to interrupt any moment because it was obvious she didn't know her lines. With a detached sense of unreality she'd heard

Adam announce she was his wife. Had he lost his mind?

"I was told to bring the woman. They didn't say anything about her husband."

"She isn't going anywhere without me." He ignored the gun in the stranger's hand as though it were a prop, adding further to Selena's sense of unreality.

The man with the gun stood there for a moment, then jerked his head. "All right, both of you." He motioned for them to continue down the hillside.

When they reached the other men, one of them said, "We're only supposed to bring the girl."

"I know. Her husband insists on coming along."

After a moment, the man with the gun said, "Come on, we're wasting time." He motioned for the other men to walk ahead of Adam and Selena, and he followed several paces behind.

They were going back to the road that Selena had followed two days before. Had it only been two days? Los Angeles seemed more than miles away—it was another life, another time. She watched Adam's shoulders as he lithely strode through the trees ahead of her. She wished she knew what was going on. She also would like to know why he had insisted on coming. His wife. What a lot of nonsense, but it had worked, she supposed. They probably would not have tolerated his being a part of this trek if they'd had any idea she and Adam barely knew each other.

The men seemed rather hostile to be government people, but maybe they were trained to be intimidating and antisocial.

Either she was getting in better condition or she was learning the way. In any event, they reached the roadway in much less time than she'd ever made the hike before. A late model Buick sat there idling with a man behind the wheel.

"Get in."

Adam stepped back and helped Selena into the back seat of the car. The other three got in and they started down the mountain.

When they turned into a side road several miles later, Selena realized that Adam had been right. Whatever was going on had something to do with her missing her turn and following a dead-end road. They drove for several miles until they reached the end of the road. Several cars were there, as well as her Ford Bronco.

"My truck!" Was the government so hard

up these days they had to steal taxpayers' cars? Under the present circumstances, she decided to wait and take it up with her Representative. These men didn't act as though they cared to debate the issue.

The car stopped and she was helped out by the driver. Adam stepped out immediately behind her and dropped his arm around her shoulder, holding her close.

"Would you like to explain why you've brought us here?"

His question was ignored.

Selena looked around the clearing. The tractor-trailer rig was pulled in alongside the trees and she realized it couldn't be seen from the air. A small trailer was almost hidden in the underbrush, and it was there the man motioned for them to go.

He opened the door and she stepped inside. There was almost no furniture in the front room and kitchen; only a couple of folding chairs and a card table stood in the bare area.

"All the comforts of home," Selena quipped, then wished once again she had better control of her tongue.

She heard the door close behind her and whirled around. She and Adam were the only ones in the room. "What's going on here?"

"You mean you haven't figured it out yet?"

"I suppose you have."

"Well, let me put it this way. I don't believe we're being held while they verify your identification."

"No?"

"No. You will notice that no one bothered to ask our names, nor did they feel the need to introduce themselves, but at least we didn't give them any trouble. Maybe they feel the deception was useful."

"What makes you think it's a deception? They seem perfectly straightforward to me. They had nothing to do with your tires being slashed or someone trying to carry me off."

Adam glanced around at her. "Is that what you think?"

"Sure. I'm certain it's just a case of accidently stumbling over a secret installation that might prove to be an embarrassment if the general public learned of it."

"You really believe these people are representatives of our government?"

"Certainly. Don't you?"

Adam didn't answer. Instead, he walked over to the picture window and peered out. After several minutes of silence, Selena's curiosity got the best of her.

"See anything interesting?"

"Too much. At least I understand why they wanted you here."

"Great. How about explaining it to me."

"The equipment on that truck is Soviet made and no doubt Soviet manned, which makes it illegal as hell in this country. They're risking a great deal having it here—so its use must be damned important."

"Soviet. How do you know?"

"I just do," he said flatly.

Selena pondered this new information for a few minutes. She didn't know why, but she felt certain Adam knew what he was talking about. A feeling of unease slipped over her.

"What do you suppose they're going to do with us?"

"Since you don't like my imaginative ideas, why don't you tell me?."

"Surely they wouldn't hurt us."

"On what vital piece of information are you basing that assumption?"

"We're innocent bystanders. They can't call us spies when we're in our own country. They have no reason to hurt us."

"Your naiveté is refreshing, but I wouldn't count on it being accurate."

Selena tentatively sat down on one of the

chairs. "This is ridiculous. All I wanted to do was to get away from spy fiction for a few weeks. So what do I do? Stumble onto a nest of them."

"I didn't exactly choose to retire here in order to find some spies myself."

"If you hadn't told them that ridiculous lie that we were married, you wouldn't even be here." She glanced up at him. "Why did you say that, anyway?"

"I lost my head. Your kiss inflamed me, your body taunted me, your—"

"Oh, shut up. You just wanted some excitement in your life and decided to horn in on mine."

"Could be. You're much more fun than Duke. At least you talk back."

"I wonder how Duke's going to get along by himself?"

"He won't be by himself for long."

"Oh, now that you know what's happening, you're going to just walk out of the place, is that it?"

"Something like that."

She shook her head. "Now I know why you live up here. If you tried to function in society, they'd have you locked away within days."

"You have a point there. Anyway, do you want to stay here or come with me?"

"You mean I have a choice?"

"Yes. I need to know what to plan. If I'm going by myself, I'll leave in a few minutes. With you along, I'll have to wait until dark."

"And then what? Are you going to grab my truck and run?"

He looked at her with a quick smile. "Come to think of it, that's not a bad idea. However, I doubt they were obliging enough to leave the keys in it."

"Even if they didn't, I know where another one is. I keep a spare hidden on the truck."

He looked at her with new respect. "Not only a beautiful face, but a brilliant brain to go with it."

"You know, Adam, I could grow to dislike you with almost no effort at all."

"And I thought we had such a great marriage going for us."

"With no effort at all," she repeated.

Adam opened the door on the other side of the kitchen and peered into the adjoining room. "Why don't you stretch out in here and rest? We may have a hard night ahead of us."

She eyed him with suspicion. "What's that supposed to mean?"

"If we can't get our hands on your truck, we're going to have a few miles to hike."

Selena followed him into the other room. A single bed and a chair were the only pieces of furniture. Remembering how early they'd gotten up and how tired she was, Selena stretched out on the bed with a blissful sigh. "All right. I'll take my nap first and get that out of the way." She determinedly closed her eyes to the sound of his soft chuckle.

He was really a most exasperating man. With obvious delusions of grandeur, he must see himself as some ace secret agent—Derringer Drake in the flesh. She reminded herself to make Clay tone down some of his tales. Some of his readers could get themselves hurt trying to live like his hero.

She fell asleep with that resolve firmly in mind.

She woke up in Adam's arms, her head tucked under his chin. Both of his arms held her close to his lean, muscular body. Stirring slightly, she pulled away from him until she could focus on his face.

The light from the small bedroom window was dim. Either it was clouding up to rain again, or she'd slept the entire day away. Neither idea appealed to her. Here she was locked up with a man she barely knew, surrounded by several men who were less than trustworthy, and she could peacefully sleep through the tension and turmoil. Obviously her nerves were in worse shape than she'd realized.

She studied Adam's face and discovered to her dismay that she continued to find him quite attractive. Reluctantly she admitted to herself that she found many things appealing about him—his crazy sense of humor, his instinctive kindness, his protective instinct that had brought him there with her.

But I have no intention of getting involved with anyone. She meant that. Selena had never gone in for meaningless relationships. She didn't care for the game playing and constant social maneuvering for status in the tinsel world she lived in. Although she enjoyed acting, she was often dismayed at the life-style that was expected of her.

She knew there were many people who erroneously assumed she'd been sleeping with Clay in order to get the part in the series. She'd grown tired of denying it. In truth, the reason their friendship had flourished was that neither of them wanted to take part in the fast-paced bed hopping that appeared so prevalent.

Clay had been honest with her from the beginning, and she had appreciated his honesty. Having one good friend was worth it. She had never regretted letting her guard down with Clay, and after he and Carolyn married, Selena felt accepted by them both.

She wondered why Clay had never mentioned Adam. But then Clay knew many people from his travels. All of his books were authentically researched, which was one reason for their popularity.

Selena was distracted from her thoughts by the slow, steady stroking of Adam's hand along her spine. Once again, electrical charges danced up and down her back—everywhere he touched her. She glanced up at him. His eyes were still closed but there was no denying he was awake.

She could feel a slight tremor in his hand and wondered at the possible effect she could be having on him. After all, he'd lived alone for some time. Sharing a bed with a woman, no matter how innocent the occasion, could have an adverse effect on him.

When she tried to pull away, his hold tightened, effectively locking her against him. She raised her head to demand that he let go of her and his mouth came down on hers in a passionate claim of possession.

None of his kisses had prepared her for the sweeping sensation of belonging to him that rose within her. Being in his arms felt so natural, so right. Her arms crept around his neck and she gave herself to the overwhelming rush of desire he caused to flow deep within her.

The sound of the front door being unlocked interruped the mood of the moment. Adam's muttered imprecations struck her as amusing under the circumstances. "What did you think you were doing just now, anyway?" she asked.

"Practicing my married role, of course."

"Of course. Frankly, I don't think you need any practice." She sat up and ran her hand over her hair. Long wisps were hanging down, and with some impatience she pulled the hairpins out of the golden mass, allowing it to tumble to her shoulders.

He ran his hand through her hair. "Oh, but I do."

She stood up. "Then you're going to have to find someone else to practice on."

The bedroom door opened and their captor stood there watching them with a smirk on his face. It took little effort to guess that he was convinced he'd interrupted something. She glanced around and saw that Adam was fostering the impression by reluctantly sitting up beside her with a frustrated frown on his face.

Men! She resented their captor's assumptions, but even more, she resented the effect Adam had on her.

"I've brought you something to eat," the man in the doorway said.

"When are you going to let us go?" Selena asked, getting up from the bed.

The man smiled—an oily smirk that infuriated her. "Soon. Probably before dark tomorrow."

"Tomorrow! You can't keep us here overnight!"

He looked around the room. "Why not? Aren't you comfortable here?" He glanced at the single bed. "I realize the bed is a little small, but as long as you're friendly, there shouldn't be a problem."

Adam saw that an eruption of Selena's temper was imminent, and he decided he'd better try to sidetrack her. "What is the purpose of our being held here?"

"This is a restricted area. Your wife was seen driving in here the other evening. We can't take any chances at the moment. A very delicate surveillance system is being tested, but the test should be through in the next twenty-four hours.''

Adam wondered if Selena was buying that ridiculous story and almost hoped she was. Their situation could become a little strained if the man discovered he was someone other than the innocent husband of the woman who'd accidentally stumbled on their little setup.

''You know, Selena, it really doesn't matter whether we're here or at the cabin—we're on vacation so we might as well relax and enjoy it.'' His smile was warm and teasing.

She stared at him as though he'd lost his mind. Being locked up in a small area with him was nothing like the vacation she had envisaged, but she hesitated to say so in front of the stranger. If she were honest, she would have to admit that his presence made the whole mess a little easier to accept. If they knew he was only an acquaintance, the chances were good that she'd find herself alone.

Which was worse? Being alone and frightened by her captors, or being with him and frightened by her reactions to him. For some reason, neither choice sounded particularly safe.

The man turned away and disappeared down the hall. They heard him say, ''I left you some sandwiches and soft drinks here in the kitchen area. See you in the morning.''

The door banged closed and they stared at each other while they listened to the sounds of his key in the lock.

''I'm not staying here with you tonight.''

''I didn't ask you to.''

''Maybe you didn't, but I don't intend to carry the deception any further.''

''I told you I plan to leave here as soon as it's dark. Do you want to go with me or wait here until I can go for help?''

She stared at him in disbelief. He was still talking like some adventure hero in a book. ''Just how do you intend to get out of here, crawl out one of the louvered windows?''

''You didn't answer my question.''

Adam no longer looked like the man who'd rested so peacefully beside her only a short time before. He looked dangerous. She could think of no other word for it. There was something quietly lethal about the way he'd made the statement that she'd missed at first.

''Can you get us both away from here?''

''Yes.''

She believed him. Despite what she felt

about him, she had a hunch he wouldn't make a definite statement unless he was sure. He sounded very sure.

She smiled. "I'll go with you. Maybe I can give Clay some technical pointers for the next escape scene he has to write for Derringer and me." Looking out at the darkening sky, she asked, "When do we go?"

"When it's completely dark—and you've changed into your other clothes."

She'd forgotten that she'd stuffed a change of clothing into her handbag. Adam walked out of the room but returned a moment later with her bag. "Why don't you go ahead and get ready and I'll see about setting out our food. We'll need to eat."

Selena pulled out her black jeans and black turtleneck sweater. A sudden excitement shot through her. She was going to be living one of the scenes she'd spent three years portraying. With Adam. Adrenaline coursed through her.

Whatever happened, she knew she was ready to follow his lead, even if she couldn't fully understand why.

Chapter Five

"Can you see anything?" Selena whispered.

"No." Adam stood by the front window, looking intently at the clearing in front of them. He'd turned off the lights in the trailer so that their eyes would adjust to the darkness.

"I wonder why there aren't any lights out there?"

"They don't want to alert anyone that they're here."

"Oh." She remembered their supper a few hours earlier. "I wonder where they got the food?"

"My guess is that someone is bringing it to whoever is up here. We know there are at least four of them. I would imagine there are more.''

''It's eerie to think so many people are nearby and we can't see or hear them.''

''Yes.''

She rubbed her hands up and down her forearms. The waiting was getting to her. ''How can you be so calm?'' she finally blurted out.

''I'm used to it. You learn to develop patience.''

Silence filled the room. Too late Adam realized what he'd said. He tried to explain. ''Living by yourself teaches you not to get impatient.''

Selena wasn't buying it, but she knew it would do her no good to ask questions. He would tell her only what he thought she needed to hear.

Adam moved away from the window in a silent step that succeeded in making her even more nervous. ''We need to wait a while yet. I'm going to try to get your truck. There's no reason to have to hike out of here when it's sitting over there waiting for us.'' She didn't say anything. ''But we'll need to wait a few more hours to try that.''

''Who are you, Adam?''

''What are you talking about?''

"I don't even know your last name...."

"Conroy."

"And I don't believe you learned your skills living in a cabin on a mountainside."

Adam ran his hand through his hair. "All right. You deserve some explanations, and I'll give them to you. But let's get away from here first." He slid his hand to the nape of her neck and began to massage the area in slow, even strokes. "Why don't you go rest for a while."

"I might as well. This conversation isn't getting us very far." She spun on her heel and strode down the hallway.

Even in the darkened room, Adam could see her lithe shape and haughty back and knew she was furious with him. If he could trust these characters, he would leave her here until he could get back tomorrow. But he didn't dare take the chance. He hoped she got over her anger before they needed to leave.

She was quite a woman. He allowed himself the luxury of a grin while he remembered her response to his kiss earlier. Talk about fiery— and passionate—and beautiful— He'd better get his mind on another subject before he followed her back into the bedroom for more.

Later Selena couldn't believe how easy it was for them to leave. She didn't know what

Adam had done to the door, but when he came to get her, he'd managed to get the door open.

The night sounds of the forest were reassuring. Adam had told her to follow closely behind him. They skirted around the clearing and, staying in the shadows of the trees, followed the road for what seemed like miles. Finally, Adam stopped.

"All right," he whispered. "You stay here. I'm going back for your truck."

"My truck! Are you crazy?" she hissed.

"Shhhh. No. It will be much more simple to get out of these mountains on wheels. I don't know how long it will take them to discover we're missing or how interested they will be in finding us once they do. The truck will get us out of here."

"But they'll hear you!"

"Probably, but by then, it will be too late to stop us. Watch for me, and be ready to jump into the truck. We won't have much time."

She nodded. Her heart was suddenly thumping in her chest. She wasn't afraid for herself, but for him. "Be careful."

He smiled. "Always." In the act of turning away, he paused, then turned back to her. Pulling her close to him, he leaned down and kissed her—a very thorough, very possessive kiss. "See you later."

Within two steps from her, he had blended with the shadows and Selena shivered. Once again she was alone. She backed up against the trunk of a tree and slowly slid down until she was resting on her heels.

She had no idea how much time had elapsed when she faintly heard a car engine start up. He'd done it! Sounds carried on the still night air and she heard shouts along with the steady drone of an engine being pushed to its limits. She ran to the roadside.

Shots rang out. *Gunfire!* "Oh, Adam," she whispered. There had been no reason for him to be involved, but he had come with her anyway. He'd done a darned good job of getting them out of the situation, but at what cost?

Headlights beamed through the trees, sweeping the curve, then straightening out and pinning her in their beam. She quickly ran to the side of the road.

Gravel flew when he slammed on the brakes. He threw the passenger door open and Selena leaped onto the seat. They took off while she scrambled for the door handle. "Are you okay?" she asked breathlessly.

He laughed—an exhilarated sound that re-assured her. "I'm fine. Just fine."

"Who was shooting back there?"

"I don't know. You can't hit much with pistols—not as far away as I was. They didn't do much, if any, damage."

Just enough. When the truck started sput-tering several miles later, Adam glanced down at the gas gauge and began to curse. "A ric-ochet must have punctured the gas tank."

"Are you sure?"

"I checked it when I first got in. You had over a half tank left. We've gone less than fifteen miles. Even Detroit manages better gas mileage than that!"

He pulled the truck over to the side of the road.

"What do we do now?"

"Get to the nearest phone. As I recall, there's a combination service station-grocery store down the road. There's a public tele-phone there. We've got to reach it."

"Why? At least now we have my truck back. Once I get the gas tank repaired, I'll be fine."

"Sure you will. Until those goons catch up with you again."

He helped her out of the truck, took her

hand and hurried her down the road. All the while he kept watching the road behind them.

"Who are you going to call?"

"An old friend of mine in Washington. I'll let him handle the matter."

She digested that in silence.

Adam suddenly jerked her hand, pulling her off the road. "Here they come. Come on, we've got to hide." They leaped over the small ditch and dived for cover just as the car stopped by their truck. Adam got up. "They'll be looking around there for a while. If we stay in the shadows and keep moving, we should be all right."

They silently raced along the side of the road, out of the range of the headlights. When they heard the car, they immediately hid again, watching as the vehicle drove by slowly. They waited until it was gone.

"What do we do now?"

"Nothing's changed. I intend to find that phone. Come on."

It seemed like hours later before they rounded the curve and saw the small glowing sign of the gasoline station. Everything was closed. "You stay here," Adam cautioned her, once again disappearing into the night.

Selena was too out of breath to debate the

issue. Whatever Adam's previous occupation, he was good. She neither saw nor heard him. Even if the men who were looking for them had been standing there, they wouldn't have seen him.

She concentrated on the phone—and blinked. He was already there, standing in the shadow of the post, holding the phone and looking like a wraith. She shook her head, wondering how he did it.

He almost scared her out of a few years' growth a few minutes later when he clamped his hand over her mouth and whispered. "Don't yell. It's me."

"How did you get behind me?"

"It doesn't matter. I knew you didn't see me. I didn't want to startle you."

"So now what do we do?"

"Wait."

"For what?"

"A ride."

"From whom?"

"Friends."

"Dammit, Adam. I've known clams who are chattier than you."

He led her deeper into the trees. He leaned against one of them and pulled her against him. "But haven't you figured it out yet? I'm a man of action."

His kiss tasted of the night, of excitement, danger and a tingle of fear. His hands slid down her spine in a sensuous exploration that caused tiny coils to tighten within her. Selena couldn't understand her reaction to him and at the moment was too caught up in the myriad sensations he evoked to even try to analyze them.

His hands slipped beneath her sweater and delicately unhooked her bra. With measured movement, he explored the slight indentation of her spine, then moved his hands around to her midriff, directly below her unbound breasts.

Selena drew a ragged sigh when he released her mouth, pulling back slightly. "Adam?"

"Hmmm?"

"Why are you doing this?"

"Doing what?"

"Distracting me."

"Is that what I'm doing?" he murmured, his mouth leaving a moist path along her cheek to the corner of her eye.

"You know very well what you're doing," she muttered.

His hands cupped the fullness of her breasts

and Selena shivered at his touch. When his mouth found hers once more she realized she didn't need an explanation. She needed him.

The sound of a car driving slowly alerted them and Adam straightened. There were no lights. He watched as it paused in the driveway of the station; the lights were flicked on and off twice, then the car remained in darkness.

"Come on. Our ride's here."

Adam grabbed her hand and they raced for the car. The passenger door opened and a low voice murmured, "Taxi?"

Selena found herself shoved to the middle of the seat, with Adam leaping in behind her. "Let's go," he said, while his arm wrapped around her and pulled her close to his side.

"Where to?"

She looked at the driver. In the shadowy car she could see no clear features, just an impression of quiet strength.

Adam leaned forward slightly to look at the driver. "Do you know this area?"

"Fairly well."

"Can you get us back up near the pass?"

The driver glanced at him quickly. "I think so, why?"

"I know a place where we can disappear for a couple of days."

Selena interrupted. "Wait a minute. We don't need to disappear. If I can get my truck repaired, I intend to forget all of this and enjoy what's left of my vacation!"

She could see Adam's smile flash in the dark and she found it very irritating.

"She doesn't have a clue, does she?" the driver offered.

Adam chuckled. "Unfortunately, no. But we'll have some time while we're waiting up there. I'll fill her in." He settled back into the seat. "My name's Adam, by the way."

"Glad to meet you. I'm Eric."

"Yes. D.G. said he was sending one of his best men to us. I'm sure you're wondering why he chose you to be a driver at this time of night."

Selena felt the driver shrug. "I've been on alert for the past ten days, waiting for a call that it was time to move. I just didn't know what form it would take."

Adam began to stroke Selena's arm, up and down slowly, softly, rhythmically, and she felt herself relaxing almost against her will.

"I think we may have triggered it. Selena happened to stumble across their setup. The situation may be premature for them—but that can only help us.''

"Yes."

"Would you two mind explaining what you're talking about?" Selena demanded.

In a soothing voice Adam murmured close to her ear. "Be patient, love, and I'll explain in a short while."

"We have visitors," Eric muttered.

Adam abruptly shifted in the seat and peered out the back window. A car with no lights was approaching, by necessity, slowly. He smiled. "Good."

"Good!" Selena stared at him.

"As long as we're still of interest to them, they don't realize others know about it. Otherwise they wouldn't waste their time." He leaned forward. "Can we gain on them without letting on we know they're there?"

Eric laughed. "I'll see what I can do." He glanced at the rear view mirror. "How much farther do we need to go?"

Adam thought for a moment. "There's a trail a couple of miles up the road from here, if you can make the curve enough ahead of them and slow down, we'll get out. If we're lucky they won't see us and will continue to follow you."

"Sounds good. I've got nothing else to do until morning. I can spend the night encouraging them to learn these mountain roads."

They're enjoying this, Selena realized. She could feel the tension in Adam—his body was almost humming with it. He'd better have some answers for her. And soon.

She could feel the pulling power of the car as it began to increase its speed along the uphill grade. There was power to spare. She was amazed at how well it hugged the road and took the corners.

Adam kept watch out the back. "No lights yet. I think they'll keep them off as long as they think we aren't aware they're following."

"How much farther?"

Adam glanced around, alert for landmarks. "There's a straightaway for about a quarter of a mile after this next curve, then the road curves sharply to the left. Just on the other side of the curve is the trail I'm thinking about."

"Okay. I'll slow down as much as I can, but you'll have to be fast."

"I know."

The straightaway helped them outdistance their pursuers, but Eric had to slow for the curve. He continued to brake until Adam opened the door, then he stopped the car. "Good luck."

"Thanks. We'll see you in a couple of days."

Eric grinned as he watched Selena scramble out of the car. She barely heard his comment as he pulled away. "Wish we could exchange jobs."

"We don't have time to stand here, let's move." Once again Adam grabbed her hand and they sprinted up the trail. Selena found herself giving thanks for her hours of aerobic workouts and gym training. She had needed them to keep in shape for her role, but only now could she appreciate what good shape she was in.

She was also aware of Adam's condition. He had looked fit enough, but his stamina astounded her. His body was a well trained machine. He moved tirelessly up the trail, sometimes by her side, other times ahead of her. But he never lost his grip on her hand.

At one point they reached a clearing and the moonlight cast a glow that was almost spellbinding. Adam paused and listened. She could hear nothing, but she waited. Eventually satisfied, he motioned with his head for her to follow him once more.

What am I doing here? she thought more than once over the next few hours. But by the time Adam had paused again, she was too tired to care.

They must have been traveling for several hours, since the moon had shifted well to the west. Selena knew they had come to a higher elevation because she was short of breath. The naked peaks of the mountains stood like sentinels along the rim of the sky. She shivered.

She was out of her element and knew it. She had no business playing hide-and-seek with these people, whatever their purpose. Oh, what she'd give for a hot bath and a comfortable bed to curl up in.

"Do you see that canyon wall?" Adam said softly, pointing past her ear.

How could she miss it? The towering, sheer cliff was almost overpowering. She nodded, too tired to speak.

"That's where we're headed. When I was doing some exploring last fall I found a cave. It will do for shelter until this deal is taken care of."

"Why couldn't we just go back to your cabin?"

"Because that's the first place they'll look."

"Why are they so interested in finding us?"

"They're afraid you know too much."

"But I don't know anything," she wailed.

"Yes, I realize that, but it no longer matters. You are in just as much danger as if you had recognized what they're up to."

"Do you know?"

"I didn't until I talked to D.G." He slid his arm around her. "Come on. We're almost there. Once you get some rest I'll tell you everything I've managed to find out."

She tossed her head in a tired semblance of her usual manner. "Don't make it sound like you're promising candy if I'll be good."

He grinned. "What would you like me to promise you?"

"Oh, go to hell!"

His laughter didn't appease her anger. She followed him down the slope, across a shallow creek, then up a slight incline until they approached the canyon wall. She was convinced they'd followed it for several miles when he paused. "There it is."

For some reason Selena had pictured a cave along the floor of the canyon. This one opened a good seven feet above it. "How do you propose to get up there?"

"Easy. I'll boost you up, then climb in after."

What she found so disgusting was that he managed to do just that, lifting her as if she were made of helium, then hoisting himself up.

When she stood up, she realized the cave was spacious. Adam flicked on a penlight and shone it around the area. The cave wasn't deep, but the floor was a fine sand, soft and silky to the touch. Selena gratefully sank down on its surface. "I may never move again."

Adam sat down near the mouth of the cave, facing the way they'd come. "Go on to sleep. I'm going to stay up for a while."

She turned around and glared at him. He was still going to be the intrepid male, watching for predators. Well, let him! She was going to sleep.

After curling up on the soft sand, Selena remembered Clay. If he'd written such a stupid plot for one of the series' episodes, she would have ridiculed him. She could hardly wait to get home to tell him of her peaceful and serene vacation in the mountains!

Chapter Six

When Selena woke up she was alone. Bright sunshine lit up the shallow cave and the day before seemed like a dream that she might have had after spending too many hours rehearsing.

Abduction? Spies? A car chase? Bullet holes in the gas tank? She sighed. Her body told her it was very real. Some of her muscles were vigorously protesting the inhumane treatment. Wearily she sat up, rubbing her back.

Where were they? She crawled over to the mouth of the cave and looked out. Adam was kneeling by a small stream several yards away. She contemplated the broad expanse of his back that was bared to the sun, while he was splashing water over his head and shoulders.

Actually, that didn't seem a bad idea. She wondered if he had thought to bring soap, then she remembered her handbag. She'd left it in the truck. It held her change of clothes, her makeup, as well as a small bar of cosmetic soap.

Who could have guessed she would be reduced to living off the land totally in such a short time? Had she been here only a few days? It felt more like years. And it felt as if Adam already was a part of her life, which was odd. They couldn't be more different. She could never picture herself living alone with a dog for months on end—she enjoyed people too much. At least, most of the time. Lately, everything had gotten on her nerves.

Selena swung over the edge of the cave and slowly let herself down. By the time she let go, she only had a couple of feet to drop. Resolutely she moved toward the stream.

"Good morning," she said cheerfully, joining Adam by the water.

He glanced around, surprised at her good humor. "You must have slept well."

"Oh, I did. Nothing like a good hike to ensure a good night's rest and whet the appetite. When do we eat?''

Her hair tumbled around her shoulders and her face was devoid of makeup. The bright sunlight illuminated her skin, searching for flaws, but revealing none. Here was a woman who needed no artificial help to enhance her beauty. Her clear, blue gaze met his with an openness that Adam found wholesome and appealing—and foreign to his way of life.

She was an innocent in the ways of the world as he knew it, and he had a sudden sharp pain somewhere inside that others were trying to take advantage of that innocence. Was there such a thing as the rape of an innocent soul and mind, impregnating it with the evils and cunning of deceit and destruction?

He had never given the matter much thought, probably because he'd been exposed to the other life so early. He had never considered the type of person he was trying to protect with his way of life.

Now he had come face to face with one, and he found it soul shaking. He didn't want her to know the sort of life he'd led until a year ago. He didn't want to see her eyes fill with revulsion when she knew more about him. Adam had grown used to the lively cu-

riosity in her eyes, the amusement, and at
times, the attraction she felt for him. He was
aware she fought against that attraction—and
with good reason.

He could bring nothing good into her life—
only fear and a possible destruction of all her
ideals. *She means too much to me to let that
happen.*

"As a matter of fact, we are going to eat,
but first, we have to clean our breakfast."

"*Clean* it?"

He pointed to a nice sized trout. "Didn't
you know? I've been up for hours planning
our meals. I managed to catch that."

"With what, Superman? Your bare hands?"

"No, as a matter of fact, I had some fishing
gear stashed up here. I got tired of carrying it
back and forth to the cabin. That's why I knew
where the cave was." He glanced around the
meadow. "The stream gets deeper not much
farther from here. I enjoy fishing."

Several hours later Selena discovered she
enjoyed watching Adam fish. Perhaps it was
because she was hungry, or perhaps it was because she enjoyed the company, but whatever
it was, the morning had flown by while she
watched him clean the fish, wrap it in some
leaves and cook it among some coals.

Now she watched him as he quietly fished for more. She hadn't asked him why they were there, who the men were who had abducted them, and what all the satellite dishes were for. Selena had discovered that she didn't care.

Sooner or later Adam would explain to her what was going on and why they were staying here, but in the meantime, she intended to relax and enjoy the sunshine and the sound of summer all around her.

Adam was across the stream from her and he glanced up. She smiled peacefully and waved her hand in a gentle salute of contentment. Had she imagined the warm look in his eyes as he gazed at her? A slight shiver ran through her. She didn't need to be reminded of his effect on her.

She had always been independent, as far back as she could remember, and she had always been an equal in her relationships with men. However, she had let Adam take over her life from the time he'd opened the door to her, bullying her, restricting her, lecturing her and taking care of her.

Yes, he'd done that. But what amazed her the most was that she had let him do all those things and had actually enjoyed his domination. She shook her head with perplexity. *I*

must be in worse shape than I thought—ready
to become the meek little woman, ready to do
her man's bidding.

Her man. Now where had that come from?
Adam wasn't the type of person that belonged
to anyone. Neither was she. But how could she
explain the rapport that seemed to exist between the two of them? She couldn't see herself blithely running off into the mountains
with any other male of her acquaintance. She
chuckled at the thought.

"What's so funny?"

Adam had crossed the stream without her
being aware of it.

"Oh, just thinking about how different my
vacation has turned out to be."

"I'm sorry."

"Why? It hasn't been your fault. If I could
follow directions—and hadn't gotten stuck—
none of this would have ever happened."

He sat down beside her, leaning back on his
elbow. His gaze scanned the meadow and she
acknowledged that he never relaxed, at least
not completely.

"How far are we from your cabin?"

"A few miles, why?"

"Because I don't understand why we can't
go there."

"D.G. advised against it. There's too much at stake to take any chances at the moment."

"Is it going to do me any good to ask who D.G. is?"

He smiled at her tone. "I used to work for him."

"And?"

"And it made sense to see if he could shed some light on what's been happening."

"Could he?"

"Yes. The area has been under surveillance. Nobody bothered to contact me because, technically, nobody knows I'm here."

"Except D.G."

"Right."

"So you blew your cover to help me."

He started laughing. "Blew my cover? What kind of talk is that?"

She didn't smile. "I know I didn't believe you at first, but I've since realized that you don't obtain your kind of skills in the import-export business. You're some sort of government agent, aren't you?"

He could feel his body tense at her words. Now was the time to convince her she was imagining things, to laugh at her conclusions. He'd struggled too long to dismiss the past and plan a new life to entrust anyone with the truth.

Adam turned on his side and stared at her. Selena was lying flat on her back, one knee pulled up, her head resting on her arm. Her clear gaze pierced him while she waited for his answer.

Slowly, he nodded. "You're right. You blew my cover."

She waited, but he said no more. A brief look of pain flowed over his features, then was gone. His face hardened, accepting the need for his admission.

"I'm sorry." The words sounded so inadequate, but they were all she could think of to say.

"So am I," he finally admitted.

"Can you tell me what's going on?"

"That equipment you saw is some sort of jamming device that could interrupt communications between the east and west coast. They're planning something out here, and when it happens, we're supposed to be blocked from communicating."

"What are they planning?"

"I don't know. I don't know if D.G. or anyone else knows, at the moment. They're working in the dark, but D.G. thought it would be better if I got you out of the way, just in case.''

She sat up. ''I see. It was D.G.'s idea that we come up here—not yours.''

He watched the slight stiffening of her supple back. ''It was his idea I hide you. I chose the location.''

''I see.''

''I doubt it,'' he muttered, gently turning her to face him.

Off balance, Selena fell toward him and he rolled with her, stopping when she was flat on her back once more. However, this time his arms were wrapped securely around her, and his body half lay on her.

When she saw his face coming closer she tried to resist the trembling feelings within her, tried to remain passive to his touch; but when his lips touched hers, it was as if a key had been turned, deep inside her, and all the emotions he evoked within her came rushing out to engulf her.

His mouth felt firm against hers, but it was the tenderness in his touch that undid her. Her lips parted slightly, an invitation he didn't refuse. His tongue softly stroked across her full bottom lip, then dipped audaciously inside—

to taste, to explore, to conquer. And she was a willing victim.

Although Adam had replaced his shirt, he'd never buttoned it and Selena ran her hands over the hair roughened surface, delighting in the feel of him. For the moment, she forgot who she was, his past, their lack of future. She could feel the quiver he gave whenever her hands discovered the tough, muscular chest pressed against her. She could hear the pounding of his heart—and when her hands slipped around him to stroke along his broad back, she heard his groan, deep in his chest.

He leaned back from her slightly, a question in his eyes and she smiled, a smile like a thousand Christmas candles, her expression loving and serene. He pulled her sweater up and over her head. She didn't resist. He unhooked her bra and carefully pushed it aside. She reached up and slowly stroked his jaw.

And when he lowered his head to kiss her breasts, her hands lovingly stroked through his hair.

Adam's ears were ringing with the rush of blood cascading through his system. He wanted her and she was willing—was more than willing. He explored her body with soft, passionate kisses, loving her with each touch of his hands and mouth. She felt so good, and he needed her so, wanted her to distraction, loved her so much.

He froze when he realized what was happening to him. There was no place in his life for love. He couldn't afford it.

Adam drew away from her, staring at her flushed face and slightly swollen mouth, the evident effects of his touch. He swallowed. Was he out of his mind? *Yes*. He shook his head, trying to clear it.

Selena stared up at him in confusion. "Adam?"

He rolled away from her, coming to his feet. "This isn't a very good idea." His gaze touched her bared chest, then met her eyes.

She flinched from the coldness of his gaze. What had happened? One moment he was making love to her, the next he was backing away. She fumbled for the clasp of her bra and hastily pulled her sweater over her head. She felt as though Adam had taken a bucket of the icy stream water and thrown it over her.

Did he think she made a habit of lovemaking? Would he even believe her if she told him she never allowed any man such liberties, and that she had given them to him willingly?

Of course he wouldn't believe her. Why should he? No one else did.

Selena slowly came to her feet and waited for Adam to say something.

"I think we need to make some ground rules about now."

She nodded. "All right."

"We're going to be up here at least another night, maybe two. I've been living up here on my own too long, I guess."

"I see. It isn't me. It would be any woman with whom you were tucked away in the mountains. Is that what you're trying to say?"

He hated to hear the slight drawl in her voice. He knew her well enough to know that her slight hesitancy masked her emotions— pain, hurt, anger... despair. But he couldn't afford to let her know how he felt about her, either. It would be disastrous for both of them.

He nodded. "Something like that."

"Well, as long as we understand each other, I'm sure we'll have no problem getting along." With forced enthusiasm she looked around the meadow. "Shall I find another cave for the night?"

"No, dammit! I believe I can control my lust for another night or two. After all, we've spent the last three nights together and you've come to no harm.''

''I appreciate your reminding me. However, for some reason I thought you were afraid that I might be overcome with lust and attack *you*.'' She gave him her most seductive look, which he really didn't need at the moment. His body was already protesting his decision, with painful results.

He turned away from her. He had to get away for a while. Glancing back, he caught an expression on her face that shook him. He *had* hurt her, dammit—the last thing he wanted. ''I think I'm going to scout around the cabin, see if anyone's been there—check on Duke, maybe bring us something to eat. Will you be all right on your own for a while?''

For a moment she wondered why she couldn't go with him. *Silly girl. He wants to get away from you, not take you with him.* Her smile flashed. ''Sure. I'll probably take a nap or something.'' She saw the look of relief on his face. Had he expected her to make a scene? ''How about bringing me a book to read if you get a chance.''

''I'll see what I can do.''

Selena stood there and watched him walk away from her. *When did I fall in love with the man,* she wondered. She didn't know. She had only recognized it when his rejection of her had stabbed her sharply with pain. Without her being aware of it, her feelings for him had crept up on her, and she knew it would take time to overcome them.

But Selena was no fool. She intended to overcome them as soon as possible.

Chapter Seven

Selena sat in the mouth of the cave, watching the patterns of light fall across the meadow. The sun seemed to be sinking more rapidly the later it became, and she wondered if Adam would make it back before dark.

Surprisingly enough, she'd enjoyed the solitude. She'd needed some time to come to terms with what was happening between her and Adam. She knew so little about him—about his background, his career—and what she did know gave her no feeling of comfort. And yet she'd gained insight into his character over the past few days. He was a protector. Even though it meant giving himself away, he had used his skills, no doubt hard earned, to see that she was safe.

He was still doing it, even when she didn't see the necessity of it.

A movement out of the corner of her eye caused her to glance toward the end of the clearing. A large animal came loping along the trail, and her heart suddenly lodged itself in her throat. With no way to protect herself, she could only hope she would remain unseen.

Hastily scooting back deeper in the cave, she turned a fearful gaze toward the intruder and sighed with relief. It was Duke.

Laughing out loud, Selena jumped down from her perch and started toward him. "Hello, there, you monstrous excuse for a house pet," she said in her most soothing tones.

Duke responded to the tone rather than the words and came bounding over to her, butting his head into her stomach. While trying to maintain her balance Selena looked for Adam. "Where's your roommate, fella? Did you leave him to fend for himself?"

Of course not. She spotted Adam stepping from the shelter of the trees. Never had anyone looked so good. Refusing to acknowledge her tremendous relief at seeing him again, she waved and started toward him.

"It looks as though you managed to survive your afternoon in the wilderness," he said with a slight smile. He'd been worried about her, anxious that no harm come to her, but now he tried to ignore that feeling.

"I can't say I was particularly productive. I fell asleep shortly after you left."

"You probably needed it." Adam swung a backpack from his shoulders and set it down in front of him.

"Well, Santa, what did you bring me?"

"All sorts of things—food, a change of clothes, a bed—"

"A bed!"

"I thought you might be more comfortable with my sleeping bag, so I brought it along."

Selena remembered that her suitcase was at the cabin, and she was touched that he had thought to bring her fresh clothing. She touched his arm. "You're marvelous, Adam." Gazing up into his silver-blue eyes, she smiled.

Adam stiffened as the warmth in her eyes kindled a fire deep within him and made a mockery of everything he'd been telling himself. He'd spent the entire day convincing himself he was only reacting to her because he'd been alone so long, but he knew better. He could have been surrounded by available women and still react more strongly to no more than the expression on her face.

He forced himself to step back casually. "I don't think we're going to have to stay here much longer. There was no sign of anyone around the cabin. I hope that means they followed the car out of the mountains last night and think we're holed up somewhere near a town."

"Then why don't we go back to the cabin tonight?"

"It's too far to go this close to dark. If you'd like, we can leave in the morning."

She glanced around the quiet little meadow. "I don't really mind staying here overnight, but what will you do for a bed?"

He smiled. "I wasn't planning to share yours, if that's what you thought."

An unbidden picture of Adam curled close to her in the confines of a sleeping bag teased her, and she could feel the heat of her body in response. "Of course not. Why, you've been the perfect gentleman throughout our adventures." She gazed up at him with innocent, blue eyes.

"Yes," he said, digging packages of food out of the pack and setting them on the ground. "That's me, all right. A perfect gentleman."

"A little testy at times, though."

He glanced up, acknowledging the dig. "True. Perhaps you'll need to drop the perfect."

They laughed and Selena wondered why her heart suddenly lifted, pleased to know they could tease and be friends. She hated the coldness that seemed to envelop Adam at times and intended to do all she could to prevent it from reappearing.

Duke was busy exploring the area, galloping through the tall grass, flushing out rabbits. "I take it Duke was all right when you got there."

"He was stretched across the front steps, dozing in the sun. Even if anyone had dared to come around, they would never have been able to get inside."

She watched the majestic way Duke prowled and pounced. He handled himself well for such a large animal. When she returned her gaze to Adam, she discovered he was building a fire and she carefully observed his technique. There was no doubt he would be able to survive, no matter how hostile the environment.

"Adam?"

"Hmmmm?"

"Tell me about yourself," she said as she sat down.

He glanced up for a moment, then continued to add small sticks to the growing flames. "What do you want to know?"

Everything. She couldn't say that—it was too revealing. "Oh, where you were born, where your family is, how you got into your line of work...that sort of thing."

He set a small grill across the rocks that formed a ring around the fire and methodically began mixing ingredients. "I was born in Corpus Christi, on the coast of Texas, and became amphibious at an early age. I was an only child—quite a surprise to my parents, who were in their late thirties when I was born."

He stopped to call Duke, who immediately responded by galloping back to them and flopping down beside Selena, almost knocking her over with his exuberance. She sat up and wrapped her arms around her knees.

"They both taught at the university, enjoyed life, and loved me with a lack of possessiveness that I never appreciated until I grew older.''

Selena pictured a young Adam with a possessive female making demands upon him. Ducking her head slightly, she smiled. No. He wouldn't want anyone attempting to run his life.

''I was lucky enough to receive an appointment to attend the Naval Academy. After I finished there, I served in the Navy, was placed in Intelligence....'' He paused, unsure of how much he wanted to reveal about his past. ''When I got out of the Navy, I was approached to join the special group I ended up working for.''

''How long ago was that?''

''Twelve years.''

''Twelve! Isn't that a long time for someone to stay in undercover work? It has to be terribly dangerous.''

''I was good at my job,'' he said in a flat tone. ''Too good.'' His face darkened at some memory.

''So you were living up here to be on the scene for whatever's happening now?''

He shook his head. ''That's the irony of what's happened. I was betrayed by a man I trusted. One of the first things you learn in this business is not to trust anyone. There's no such thing as friendship. I made an exception in his case and almost got myself killed. I knew I'd been in the business too long, and after discussing it with D.G., we let the rumor travel that I had, in fact, been killed, along with several others, including the double agent. D.G. helped me assume a new identity and find the cabin to recuperate in, and he closed my file. Until I called him last night, we'd not been in contact. He knew I wanted it that way and he'd respected my privacy.''

"He must have been surprised to hear from you."

"You could say that." He smiled at some unspoken memory.

"Yet he allowed you to involve yourself."

"If you'll remember, I was already very much involved before I called him."

"But only because you insisted on coming along as my husband."

"I know."

"Why, Adam?"

He gave her a long look. The soft flames from the open campfire provided the only light around them. "I don't know."

Was that the truth or did he prefer to keep

his reasons to himself? Regardless, she knew he would not tell her.

"Are you ready to eat?" he asked, interrupting the silence several moments later.

"Yes. I'm starved."

Never had a meal tasted so good—the slight smokiness enhanced the flavor. Selena watched Adam feed the remaining scraps to Duke, feeling guilty she'd eaten so much.

"Have you always wanted to be an actress?" Adam stretched out on his side facing her, the warm fire compensating for the slight chill in the mountain air.

"As far back as I can remember. I used to dress up in all sorts of costumes and emote by the hour. It's a wonder my family put up with it."

"How big a family?"

"Just me—another only child."

"So you learned to entertain yourself."

"Yes. I lived in a fantasy world all my own, peopled by my favorite characters, ones I'd found in books."

"I bet you were very popular." He could see a young Selena dazzling all the boys with that smile and those sparkling blue eyes.

She laughed. "Hardly. I was the tallest one in my class through most of grade school—

felt like a giraffe. In my fantasies I was always dainty, petite, looking up to all the males around. But that's all it was—fantasy.''

"But when you were acting, you became someone else."

"Exactly."

"When did you decide to make it a career?"

"By the time I reached high school, the boys were beginning to catch up to my height, but I continued to spend my spare time doing plays. In fact, I won a college scholarship because of a one-act play contest I had entered during my senior year of high school."

"So you went to college, graduated, and became a star."

"Not quite. I went to college, graduated, and spent several years trying to get a break into the theatre."

"That's right. You mentioned that television hadn't been your first choice."

"True. But I'm not sorry I got involved with this series. It's just that I wasn't prepared for the type of publicity I received."

"Which was?"

"Sex symbol. Giant posters with a great deal of me showing. Interviews that were more interested in who I was sleeping with than my opinion of the world around me. You know the sort of thing.''

Adam grinned. ''I'm afraid not. I've never spent much time in your highly visible field. I'm embarrassed to admit I've never seen you on television, but then I haven't spent much time in this country for the last several years.''

''There's nothing embarrassing about that. Despite what the network executives would like us to believe, the nation does not revolve around what's being shown on television these days.''

''I'd like to see you, though.''

''You're welcome to come to the studio and watch us film if you'd like.''

He thought about the possibility of seeing Clay again. He was one of the few people who knew who he was—or at least who he'd been. ''We'll see.''

Selena could hear the change in his voice and realized that she'd accidentally touched on a sensitive area. Damn.

''Well,'' she said as she stretched, trying to sound unconcerned, ''I think I'll make good use of that bedroll and turn in. Are we going to sleep in the cave?''

''We can, or if you'd prefer, we can stay down here by the fire.''

"Oh, I'd much prefer the fire."

He stood and picked up the bedroll, flipping it open and spreading it a safe distance from the fire. "All the comforts of home."

"Except for a shower."

"I can't provide a shower, but we can certainly see that you have a hot bath when we get back to the cabin."

The thought of soaking in a hot bath sounded heavenly. "That's an offer I won't let you forget."

Adam sat down by the fire again, and she thought he looked so lonely, staring into the flames. She wished she knew what to say or do to take that look away. "Adam?"

He glanced up, waiting.

"Thank you for looking after me so well."

His gaze seemed to burn into her, and she felt a melting sensation begin deep within. Impulsively, she leaned over to kiss him. She meant it to be light, affectionate, appreciative; but when she felt the firm mouth pressed against hers, she forgot her original intentions. Instead, she lingered for a moment, only one short moment out of time, and was borne away into another realm of being, where loneliness didn't exist and strong attraction between two very different people was not only acceptable but pure pleasure—and to be tenderly nurtured and encouraged.

Adam's arms snaked around her waist and gently tugged until she tumbled into his lap. Her hands hesitantly explored the rugged contours of his face, her lips brushing against his, softly but insistently. When his hands buried themselves in her tumbled mass of hair, forcing her mouth even closer to his, she relaxed against him, wrapping her arms around his back.

"Oh, Selena," he murmured, his harsh breathing confirming what she already knew—he wanted her and she wanted to fulfill that desire. She wanted to give him all of herself, to bathe him in her love, to bring him comfort and care. Her kiss promised him all of these things, and he groaned with the knowledge of her willingness.

Without breaking contact, he rolled, placing her on the floor beside him as he feverishly lifted the sweater from her. His hands fumbled at the snap and zipper of her jeans, and she lifted her hips, helping him to slide them off her.

He saw her shiver and scooped her up in his arms, carrying her to the sleeping bag and gently placing her inside. As though he'd been away from her too long, he stretched out beside her and began to kiss her again—mind drugging, soul searching kisses that claimed her for his very own.

His hands roamed freely from her shoulders, touching her lightly as his palm skimmed across the pink crest of her breast, down across her stomach and abdomen. Everywhere he touched, tiny sparks exploded within her. He explored the contour of her hips and thighs and returned to the soft lace framing her bikini panties.

"Are you protected, love?" he whispered, his breath caressing her ear.

Selena's eyes blinked open as she was brought abruptly down to earth by his sensible, realistic question. She forced herself to focus her gaze on his face. The stern control he was exercising showed in the tautness of his expression.

"Oh, Adam, no, I'm not. I never needed to be before and I never dreamed I'd find someone like you..."

Her incoherent murmurings flicked across him like razor sharp whips. "You mean you've never—"

She shook her head, discovering how shy she felt even to discuss it after the years she'd spent being surrounded by people who automatically assumed...

Adam sat up, the control he'd maintained causing him to tremble. He flipped the top of the bedroll over her, then grabbed the zipper and brought it up the side. She was effectively locked away from him.

Selena tried to sit up, feeling like a mummy ready for entombment. She struggled to free her hands and reached for Adam. "Don't be angry, Adam, please."

"Angry?" He looked at her in surprise. "Dammit, Selena, I'm not angry. What I'm feeling right now is much more uncomfortable than anger! But why did you let me go on as though you intended to go through with it?"

"I didn't intend to stop you," she admitted in a low voice.

He sat beside the bedroll and stared at her, bewildered. With her looks and her profession, he knew she could only be in an untouched state through choice—her choice. And yet she'd been willing—even eager—to forget all of that with him.

His thoughts shook him. The possible explanations astounded him. They also scared the hell out of him.

He had never made a commitment to anyone in his life. Until meeting Selena, he had never given a thought to the idea. Not only his life-style and occupation but his very nature precluded his spending his life with anyone.

The fire had died down, only occasionally shooting up enough to give light. He saw the bewildered look on her face. Whatever chemical reaction was caused whenever the two of them drew close to each other, it should be labeled EXPLOSIVE. She seemed to be as confused by it as he was.

Never had Adam felt quite so old. He pushed himself up, his body protesting. His body knew exactly what he needed, but he was moving in the wrong direction.

"Try to get some sleep. We'll go to the cabin first thing tomorrow. D.G. said he'd see about having my tires replaced. As soon as that's done, I'll help you get back to town."

She nodded, not trusting her voice. Now that he knew she had no experience, he didn't want her. The irony of the situation was almost laughable, if she'd been in the mood. For the first time in her life, she'd met a man she loved enough to want to make love to, and he wasn't interested because she was a novice.

Nobody would believe me if I told them. Silent tears trickled down her cheeks while she waited for sleep to blot the past hour from her mind. *You may be a sex symbol to the rest of the nation, but you just flunked the course here.*

Chapter Eight

When Adam awoke, the sky was growing light. Only the strongest stars showed their positions in the sky and they were rapidly fading. As usual, as soon as his eyes opened he was instantly alert. He noted that Selena was still asleep—only the top of her golden hair showed over the sleeping bag.

Duke snored peacefully nearby, used to nights spent out in the open. When Adam first came to the mountain, he'd spent more time outdoors than inside the cabin. He'd fought the phobia of confinement by sleeping under the stars. Many nights he'd lain awake, fighting sleep and the ensuing nightmares that had haunted him for months.

Sometime during the winter months, so imperceptibly as to be unnoticed, he'd begun to accept the healing balm of sleep. Slowly his mind had let go of the unspeakable horrors he'd witnessed and allowed them to be buried deep within him.

He'd been deathly tired of his life-style—of striving, of battling the outlandish odds. The mountains had welcomed him, and although he hadn't realized it until now, they had healed him. The physical scars he carried were only a small portion of his total injuries. He'd accepted the fact that he would be emotionally crippled for the rest of his life.

And then Selena appeared in his life, her off-beat sense of humor startling and intriguing him, her ability to accept and deal with inexplicable incidents surprising him. There were no shrill demands, no hysteria.

When had he fallen in love with her? He wasn't even sure. Perhaps while she stood before him, drenched, her blue eyes meeting his without flinching, her delicate chin raised slightly to meet courageously whatever was happening to her. Or was it when he first kissed her after finding her unconscious not far from his doorstep?

He recalled his moment of panic when he

first saw her—not another death for him to
deal with; it was too soon. He recalled his relief when he discovered she was alive and rel-
atively unharmed.

But when he realized she was giving herself
to him totally last night, when she'd never
given herself to anyone before, he'd been
overwhelmed by his love for her.

The question was: what the hell was he going to do about it?

He had nothing to offer her. His skills were
not the most marketable in a legitimate world.
Since he'd invested most of his earnings over
the past several years, he didn't need to work
to survive, but he couldn't very well offer a
Hollywood actress the rare treat of living in a
mountain cabin with a self-styled hermit for
the rest of her life.

He wasn't at all sure he could even function
in the society in which she dwelled. Even if
he could, would he want to?

The mountains to the east were black sil-
houettes and the soft clouds above them began
to turn shades of purple and vermilion. Adam
lay quietly watching as nature's canvas took
on the varied colors of dawn in rapidly chang-
ing patterns.

* * *

Selena was being chased by faceless pursuers. She was running down a narrow, winding road, and the trees were leaning closer and
closer, reaching out long limbs to snag at her.
She was running out of breath but she had to
keep running. She could hear them panting behind her…panting…

She sat up with a start. Duke sat up by her
side, his wide mouth grinning, his tongue loll-
ing as he watched the terror in her eyes gradually recede.

"You dumb dog! You scared me to death."

He lifted his paw for her to shake.

"And don't try to change the subject." She
looked around her and noted a new fire burning but no sign of Adam. "What are you doing
here, anyway? Why aren't you with your
friend?"

Duke cocked his head slightly, seemingly
puzzled by her question.

"Never mind." The sun felt good on her
arms. She glanced at her watch and was surprised to discover it was after eight o'clock.
She must have slept for hours, rejection not-
withstanding.

A drifting thought circled then danced
away, and she smiled. She had pictured herself
going to Adam and offering to run home and

get some experience if he promised to wait until she got back.

No. That probably wouldn't work. She knew it wasn't because he didn't find her attractive. The high voltage electricity generated between them could not be all one-sided. Besides, his body had shown physical evidence that he was quite able to carry their lovemaking to its inevitable conclusion. Only *he* wasn't willing.

I wonder if I should try to seduce him? She had no trouble playing that type of role— mostly because the writers told her exactly what to do. Besides, the actors always knew how to respond. Without a script, she was helpless. Well, maybe not as much helpless as unimaginative.

She sighed.

Oh, well, life goes on. She unzipped the bag and suddenly remembered, as the cool morning air hit her nice, warm body, that she had slept only in her briefs. Adam was quite proficient at stripping her down to the basics with a few economical movements.

He'd said he'd brought her a change of clothes. Gingerly stepping across the dew dampened grass, Selena dug into the backpack for his promised treat.

Adam had caught a nice string of fish for breakfast. He was almost within hailing distance of their campsite when he noticed Selena was stirring. She was kneeling by his pack and obviously found what she was looking for because she let out a satisfied "Hah" and stood up.

He froze, one foot a few inches off the ground. The sunlight gilded her body; she was clad only in the tiniest excuse for panties he'd seen, and he suddenly understood why her promoters had considered life-size posters.

Her body was flawless. From her smoothly shaped shoulders and arms to her saucy breasts, flat stomach and gently swelling hips, she could have modeled for one of the Renaissance painters or sculptors. Her long legs were shapely and firm, and Adam discovered that his racing pulse and shortness of breath were becoming a problem.

He managed to turn around and gaze back the way he'd come, taking slow, deep breaths, and he reminded himself that his stay on the mountain had turned him into a healthy, normal human being. His reaction to her was certainly proof of that.

After waiting for several minutes, he slowly turned around again—and breathed a sigh of relief. Selena was completely clothed and sitting by the fire, warming her hands and talking to Duke.

Duke was the first to see him. Barking joyously, Duke ran over to his master, gamboled around him and darted back to Selena. She began to laugh at his antics.

"He's a real clown, isn't he?"

"At times," Adam admitted. He held up the string of fish. "How about some breakfast. Are you tired of fish?"

"No. That sounds great. Shall I help?"

"There's not much to do. If you want to dig out the skillet I brought and get it ready, I'll have these cleaned shortly."

They ate in companionable silence. Selena had been afraid Adam would be cool and formal with her, after what had happened—or almost happened—the night before. Instead, he seemed relaxed and casually friendly.

"Do you ever get down to Los Angeles?" she asked while they cleaned up after breakfast.

"I've flown in and out of the airport—that's about all."

"If you're ever down that way, I hope you'll give me a call. I'll be glad to show you around."

Adam smiled. "If I'm ever down that way."

"Okay, so most hermits don't do much traveling, but even a hermit needs a vacation once in a while. Look at me. I work around people all the time, so I vacation in the solitude of the mountains. You spend all your time in the mountains, so it makes sense you'd vacation where there are people."

"Sounds logical."

"Of course it does." She looked around the site, noting that Adam had carefully put out the fire and scattered the ashes. "Are we ready to go?"

"Just about." He finished repacking his backpack and settled it easily on his shoulders. "Let's go."

The hike back covered some rough terrain, and Adam did it in easy stages.

"I had no idea it was so far," Selena finally admitted, sinking gratefully to the ground.

"It really isn't all that far, but we have to go in a round about way to get there. We almost could have seen the cabin from the ridge overlooking the meadow we were in. But we have to make a loop in order to get there."

"At this rate, I should be in great shape

when I get home." She felt along her calf where pains were shooting.

"There's nothing wrong with your shape," he muttered, thinking of the early morning view.

Selena blushed, remembering how she'd encouraged him to strip her the night before. He must think she was shameless. Come to think of it, she almost was where he was concerned. She couldn't understand how he'd become so important to her so quickly.

"We should be there in another hour. Think you can make it?"

"Of course. Lead on, oh mighty leader."

For the rest of the hike, Selena kept going only by recalling the promised hot bath. Once she got inside the tub, she'd never crawl out again.

Never had one small cabin looked so good. Duke loped ahead of them, systematically checking to see if there had been visitors since he'd left. He obviously was satisfied with his inspection because he came bounding back to them. Selena wished she had some of his energy.

Adam unlocked the door and, after making a motion for her to wait, stepped inside. After carefully scanning the room, he nodded for her to come in. His habits were so ingrained she doubted he was even aware of them.

I wonder if he will ever be comfortable living in our society, she mused. The increased crime rate and the public's apparent helplessness in combating it made his skills useful, but dangerous.

"I'll put some water on to heat and fill a tub for you, if you'd like."

She smiled warmly at him, touched by his thoughtfulness. "That sounds wonderful." She sank down into the chair by the table and pulled off her boots. Flexing her toes with a sigh of pleasure, she watched as he pumped the water, set it on the stove and started a fire.

"I'm afraid it will take a while to get hot."

"I don't mind, as long as you don't have somewhere else for me to hike to."

He laughed. "No. While you're bathing I'm going to check on the Jeep to make sure the tires were changed. I was hoping to find a message somewhere that everything has been taken care of."

"What do you expect to happen?"

"No one is sure. Right now our visitors are being monitored. They're planning something—something big—but you are no longer involved."

"How did that happen?"

"We gave them the slip. By now they realize it."

"But won't they look for us here?"

"I'm sure they did, just as I'm sure all roads leading into this area are under their surveillance. But I'm fairly certain they're convinced you're long gone from here."

She nodded. "I've discovered that I much prefer my intrigue and spy stories as a script, nothing more. I don't know how you've managed to live that sort of life."

"It gets to you after a while. Either you become as cold and callous as the people you're dealing with, or it begins to eat deeply into your soul."

"You didn't become hard."

His gaze fastened intently on hers. "I did, but eventually even I couldn't stomach the reality of my life. I had to get out."

"Do you intend to live up here permanently?" she asked, looking around the room with affection.

"I haven't thought that far ahead. It was enough that I had a lair to hide in while my body healed and my mind attempted to find its way back to civilized thinking."

"I'm so sorry that I brought all of it back to you."

He slowly walked over to her and placed his hands lightly at her waist. "I'm not. I'll never be sorry for having the chance to meet you—to get to know you." His mouth gently brushed against hers. "You're really a very special person."

Selena relaxed in his arms and he drew her closer to him, his kiss softly searching, a careful restraint. She knew he had no intention of deepening their relationship.

Did she?

Of course not. She had her own life, a flourishing career and good friends. Regardless of how deeply her feelings ran for him, Adam wanted nothing from her but friendship. That was enough. It would have to be.

Adam glanced over at the stove. "Your bath awaits, milady," he said with a smile. He pulled out an oversized, oblong tub that had been stored underneath the kitchen cabinets. With deft movements he poured the boiling water into the tub, adding cold water from the pump until the water level rose to a satisfactory point.

"Why don't you go ahead and relax. I'm going to check on the Jeep. If we have wheels, perhaps I can get you out of here today. I'm sure you're ready to rejoin the civilized world by now.''

After he left, Selena stood staring at the door. The thought of leaving him was repugnant to her, and she had to remind herself firmly that he was a friend—a *friend*.

Stripping off her grubby clothes, Selena crawled into the tub with a sigh of sensuous enjoyment. Nothing could feel better than the deliciously warm water flowing so smoothly against her tired muscles. She leaned her head back and closed her eyes.

The cooling water finally convinced her she had to get out and dress. Adam's absence was definitely going to draw to a close shortly, and she didn't want to embarrass either of them by still being in the tub when he returned.

After drying herself, she found clean jeans and a tank top to put on. It was time to go looking for him.

She didn't have to go far. Just as she rounded the corner, she saw him coming up from the trail leading to the road. She waved. "I thought I was going to have to send Duke out to find you," she called.

His grin lit up his face as he took in her well scrubbed appearance. "Hardly. I discovered I was getting hungry and thought I'd come back and dump you out if I had to, so I'd have room to prepare a meal.''

He lengthened his stride, but he was still some distance away when he heard a gunshot and saw Selena suddenly spin and fall to the ground. A second shot whined past his ear, and he rolled to the ground. The ambush was coming from the trees opposite the front door of the cabin.

Staying low, he rapidly crawled to where Selena lay. Blood poured from a wound in her side and she was unconscious.

The bitter curses that fell from his lips had no power to undo the damage. He measured the distance to the cabin. He had enough weapons in there to repel an attack, but the most important thing was to get Selena to a doctor. She needed immediate help.

Another burst of gunfire brought an answering volley from somewhere close by, and Adam saw Eric and two other men closing in. Help had arrived, but he wondered if it were too late to help Selena.

He felt for her pulse. It was weak but still discernible. Carefully gathering her in his arms, he started back down the hill. Two cars were pulled up beside the Jeep with one man standing nearby.

"We've got to get to a hospital—right now!"

The man swung around and climbed into the closest car. "Get in. I'll get you there as soon as I can."

Adam had no conception of time as he held Selena in his arms during that long drive out of the mountains. She whimpered and he leaned down to her ear. "You're going to be all right, darling. I won't let anything harm you."

But he had. He had stood there, unable to prevent her being shot.

Her eyes flickered open. "Adam?" she whispered.

"Yes, love. I'm here. We're going to the hospital right now."

"What happened?" Her voice was barely audible.

"I'm afraid I was a little too smug. I thought we'd beaten them—but they found us after all."

"My side hurts. It feels like it's on fire."

"I know, love, I know. Just take it easy." He pulled her closer to him, nestling her head into his shoulder.

Had trouble followed him or was it all just a ghastly coincidence? He couldn't allow himself to consider that Selena had received a bullet intended for him. That way of thinking lay madness.

Adam strode through the emergency entrance of the small county hospital with Selena in his arms and was met with professional efficiency. Within minutes she was being prepared for surgery. The bullet had lodged itself in her side. A higher calibre bullet might have ripped a hole in her back as it went through.

He refused to consider that she might not recover.

Selena hurt. Her side felt as if it had been sandblasted. Her throat was so dry she could barely swallow, and her lips felt parched. If only her eyelids didn't weigh so much she'd get up and get a drink of water.

Why did her side hurt so much? Had she fallen? She remembered the long hike with Adam back to the cabin, but she didn't remember falling.

"Adam..." she murmured.

She heard someone shift in a chair nearby, and a hand reached out and gently touched hers. "I'm here, love."

Selena tried to force her eyes open without success. Had the makeup woman glued them together or something? When was the last time she'd had a drink? "So thirsty," she mumbled.

A sliver of ice was placed on her lips and it tasted delicious. Eagerly she opened her mouth for more, her tongue touching the cold piece with greedy desire.

"Does that help?" His voice was barely audible.

She tried to nod but her head wouldn't cooperate. Adam picked up her hand and laid it against his cheek. She could feel the beginnings of a beard. When had he last shaved? She'd have to tease him about his Grizzly Adams appearance.

If only she could get her damned eyelids to work. Maybe if she had someone trim the eyelashes—would that make them lighter? She was still trying to decide, when she fell asleep once more.

The next time she woke up, her eyes were much more cooperative. She gazed around the small room with vague curiosity. The decor left a great deal to be desired. Pale green walls surrounded her. A small window was shuttered against the light by aging venetian blinds. There were two chairs in the room—one against the wall near the door, the other pulled up beside the bed. The one by the bed was occupied.

Selena turned her head for a better view. Adam was asleep, his head resting on the back of the chair, his body lounging. He looked awful. He hadn't shaved in days, and his clothes were rumpled. He looked nothing like the Adam she knew.

He still looked wonderful to her, though. She wondered why they were there. The room had very little going for it. The least he could have done was found a room with two beds. Poor man—he looked exhausted.

The door whispered open and Selena fought to change the focus of her eyes. Why did it seem that everything she did was in slow motion? A young woman in a white, zippered jacket walked in. She wore a nursing cap on her dark hair. *Aha. My powers of observation have not deserted me in my time of need. That woman is a nurse. It would be a safe assumption to believe that we are in a hospital.*

Selena was proud of herself. A tidy piece of deductive reasoning if she'd ever experienced it. She tried to smile but her lips felt as if they'd crack into a thousand tiny pieces.

The nurse took her pulse then checked her blood pressure and temperature with equipment that looked like something out of a science fiction movie. Digital readouts flashed on, and she quickly jotted them down. With efficient movements, the nurse slightly shifted Selena, picked up a syringe and deftly inserted the needle into Selena's hip. She was surprised to discover the shot had been painless and smiled her appreciation.

Both women glanced at the sleeping man and refrained from speaking. Selena tentatively licked her lips, and the brilliant nurse poured her a small amount of water on cue. Either she could read minds or most patients woke up thirsty. Someday she'd have to ask her.

Patting Selena's hand, the nurse turned around, looked at Adam with a slight smile and departed.

Selena went back to sleep watching Adam. When she woke up again, he was gone.

Chapter Nine

Selena lay there wondering where Adam could have gone and wished she hadn't slept so soundly that she hadn't heard him when he left.

The door opened and she eagerly watched to see who came in. Another nurse entered, carrying a tray. "Good morning. I've brought you something for breakfast. Are you hungry?"

Selena didn't know. She felt as though she were floating several inches above the bed and wondered if the shot the other nurse had given her could have something to do with the sensation.

"Where's Adam?" Her voice sounded raspy, and she tried to clear her throat.

"Adam? Oh, you mean your friend? I saw him leave about an hour ago. Probably needed to get cleaned up." She smiled at Selena. "He hasn't left your side since you were brought out of recovery."

"Recovery?"

"Yes. They had to remove the bullet that hit you."

Interesting. A bullet had hit her. She tried to recall when it could have happened. She remembered her sinfully long bath and her going out to look for Adam. She even remembered his loping stride up the incline toward her. What then?

She must have been shot. "Was Adam hurt?"

"Devastated, from what I could see."

"I mean, was he shot?"

"No. But I've never seen a man so beside himself when he brought you in."

"How long have I been here?"

"Three days."

"Three!" It didn't seem possible. No wonder he'd looked tired. She hoped he would be back soon.

After a breakfast of clear broth and hot tea,

Selena slept until early afternoon. When she drowsily opened her eyes, Clay Kenniwick sat in the chair next to the bed, studying her.

Clay was not tall but had the heavy chest and arm muscles of a wrestler. His golden beard was sculpted to a strong jawline, but his beard couldn't conceal the broad grin when she opened her eyes.

"It's about time, Goldilocks."

"Have I been sleeping in your bed?" she asked plaintively.

His grin turned into a chuckle. "Not likely. Carolyn would never understand." He glanced around the room in disgust. "This was not what I had in mind when I suggested a quiet, restful vacation."

"It wasn't? I don't understand why not. I have all the comforts of home, my meals brought on a tray. I don't have to lift a finger."

"The question is, *can* you lift a finger?" One eyebrow lifted in a quizzical gaze.

"Come to think of it, I haven't tried." Selena glanced down at her hand lying on the white sheet and tentatively wriggled her fingers. With a triumphant expression, she said, "There. I can lift a finger with ease."

He leaned over and kissed her on her forehead. "I'm very glad to hear it. How are you feeling?"

"Like I've been shot. I had no idea it felt so awful. The television series always makes it look so heroic when a person is shot and he is still able to wipe out the enemy before the commercial. It's not only heroic, it's impossible!"

"Have they told you we're moving you?"

"We?"

He didn't meet her gaze. "The powers that be felt you should be closer to home. You're going to be flown back to Los Angeles."

"But what about Adam?"

"Who?"

"Adam Conroy. You remember him, don't you?"

Clay shook his head. "Am I supposed to?"

"He said he knew you—that you'd met several years ago in the Far East."

He smiled. "I've met a lot of people, Selena, my love. I can't remember all of them."

"Oh." She couldn't help feeling a little disappointed, but she wasn't sure why.

"Is this Adam fellow the one who brought you in?"

"Yes. He was trying to save me from some

spies who had satellite dishes set up in the woods near his cabin and—"

"Whoa...wait a minute. Whatever they're giving you for pain is making you a little spacey."

"No, it's not the medication. You just wouldn't believe what's been happening."

He could see she was growing agitated. He took her hand and deliberately changed the subject.

"Carolyn sent her apologies for not flying up with me, but right now she's having an uncomfortable bout with morning sickness."

The diversionary tactic worked. "Morning sickness. Carolyn?"

He grinned, his blue eyes dancing with a devilish gleam. "Umhmmmm."

"I take it you aren't too upset by that unexpected turn of events."

"Not really. We had talked about a family in another few years but...what can I say? I have a tough time keeping my hands off the lady."

Selena smiled, thinking of the way they'd met. Carolyn had given him a tough time from the very beginning. She didn't know anyone who deserved it more! "I suppose that will cut down on some of your traveling for authentic details…at least for a while, won't it?''

He shrugged. ''Probably, but I've got enough data to draw on for several more novels and a few dozen more television episodes. I'm not too worried.''

Selena shifted restlessly in bed and Clay tensed. ''Are you in pain?''

She grimaced. ''A little. I was just wondering why Adam hadn't returned. I hate to leave without at least thanking him for saving my life.''

''Does he live somewhere nearby?''

''Hardly. He lives like a hermit on top of one of the mountains with a Great Dane.''

''Are you sure he intended to come back?''

The innocent question smashed into her with unexpected force. What made her think he'd be back? Was it because he'd stayed by her side for three days and nights?

''I don't know,'' she finally admitted.

She was so pale. Clay had never seen her like this and it worried him. He stood up, taking her hand. ''You can always drop him a line to thank him once we get you home.''

''Yes.''

''Look, you try to get some rest, and I'll

make the final arrangements for the transfer. You'll be your old self in no time.''

She nodded, her weighted eyelids drooping. She felt so dopey. Maybe when she woke up again, Adam would be there. Selena went to sleep with a slight smile on her face.

Adam sat staring into the empty fireplace, Duke's chin resting on his knee. Selena seemed to haunt him. He remembered so much about her—the way the sunlight highlighted her hair, the warm blond waves dancing as she hiked along the trail, the sound of her infectious laughter when she was amused, and she found so much about life to amuse her.

Her enjoyment of life and her ability to see the humor in almost any situation seemed totally foreign to him. For too long his survival had depended on his facing the grim facts of life. He'd never had time to relax and enjoy the common, everyday occurrences. He felt as though Selena had introduced him to a whole new perspective on life. He missed her.

How could someone become such a necessary part of his life in a few short days? At least he was going to be honest with himself. His love for her was what ate at him.

He got up and strode to the door, jerking it

open. The calm vista that had been a soothing balm over the past months beckoned to him. Snapping his fingers for Duke, he waited for the dog, then closed the door and stepped outside.

He had to decide what to do. Or had he unconsciously made his decision when he left the hospital without speaking to her again? The doctor assured him she was out of danger, and he knew if he stayed any longer, he'd tell her how he felt about her.

He started up the trail to the meadow where he'd spent so many enjoyable hours fishing. Maybe that activity would be a panacea for him once again.

He knew he had nothing to offer her. They didn't even have that much in common. She would probably burst out laughing if she knew how he felt about her. She had everything in her life in order, and once she returned home she would no doubt quickly forget about him. He wished he believed he could forget her. All he could do was try.

Selena's hospital room in Los Angeles looked considerably different from the county hospital. Warm colors covered the walls, and the room had so many flowers in it that she wondered if she should open a florist's shop.

Everyone had been so kind. The doctor assured her she was progressing satisfactorily, so she couldn't understand why she was so depressed.

Her mind continued to dredge up memories of Adam. Why couldn't she forget him? He'd watched out for her, taken care of her, and according to the hospital staff, rushed her to emergency and sat with her until she was safely out of danger.

Then he'd left.

She couldn't understand why she'd grown so close to him in such a short time, but she felt as though she'd known him forever. He'd made it clear he wasn't affected in the same way.

The door quietly opened and a young woman with short, black hair and sparkling, black eyes peered around the door.

Selena smiled, glad to have her thoughts interrupted. "Come on in, Carolyn. It's good to see you."

Carolyn's warm smile lit up the room. "It's great to see you looking so good. Clay said you really scared him when he first saw you— you were so pale."

"The trouble with Clay is, he's never seen me without my makeup. That's my usual early-morning look—as though I'm ready to take my last breath." She took in Carolyn's radiant look. "For someone suffering from morning sickness you look remarkably healthy."

Carolyn perched on the chair by the bed. "Oh, I'm doing better. The doctor gave me some medicine to take."

"Well, I want you to know I'm pleased for you two."

"Thank you. Clay took the news better than I expected."

"Don't kid yourself. That man is so proud, the buttons on his shirt kept threatening to explode when he told me." She watched the woman who'd managed to wrap the elusive Clay Kenniwick around her little finger and was amazed that Carolyn still didn't recognize the power she had over him. Selena had enjoyed watching their courtship and marriage these past two years and was determined not to settle for less than what those two shared.

Adam's face appeared in her mind and she almost groaned. *Will you go away and quit haunting me?*

"Are you still in much pain?" Carolyn

asked sympathetically, and Selena realized she must have been scowling.

"No, not really. I asked them not to give me any more shots for pain—I felt too disoriented. But the tablets take care of it."

"The news media is reporting that you were shot in a hunting accident. What happened?"

"I really don't know. I had intended to ask Adam but he never came back to the hospital."

"Who's Adam?"

"The man I was with."

"Sounds interesting, tell me more."

"I don't think I can talk about him right now, Carolyn. Someday, maybe."

"Oh my. You must have really fallen for him."

"'Fraid so. You'd think I'd have more sense."

"If you love him, he must be quite a man. You don't give your love lightly."

Selena stared at Carolyn in confusion. Where had she gained that insight about her? Perhaps she was right. She had met men who were suitably eligible and who confessed to worshiping her and wanting to marry her—but she could never commit herself.

What had been so different about Adam?

She didn't understand it herself, and she found it downright aggravating.

"I know you're tired, and I need to run a couple of errands. Take care and I'll be in to see you tomorrow." Carolyn paused by the door. "Do you know when they intend to release you?"

"Toward the end of the week, I understand."

"Sounds good. See you later."

Selena lay there staring at the door for a long time after Carolyn had left, wishing she could get excited about going home, going back to work, returning to her life-style. Somehow, none of it seemed to matter any more.

Clay hung up the phone and turned to Carolyn who was next to him, curled up in their massive bed.

"You'll never guess who that was."

Carolyn yawned. It was almost eleven. Normally she'd still be wide awake but her pregnancy kept her chronically drowsy.

"Who?"

"Adam."

Carolyn sat up with a bounce. "*Selena's* Adam?"

"Yep."

"What did he want?"

"He wanted to know how Selena was doing."

"And you told him…"

"I told him her recovery had been slow and that we were concerned about her."

"But Clay, she's making an excellent recovery, you know that!"

He grinned. "Physically, yes."

"Oh ho. Now who's playing matchmaker?"

"Not me. I just think it's interesting that he's so concerned. He filled me in on what happened up there. What he didn't tell me was even more interesting."

"Are you sure you're not reading something into the situation?"

"Hardly. The man I knew would never have bothered to check on anyone, once he knew she was going to survive."

"I didn't realize you knew him."

"That's because I knew him under another name. You don't forget a person who once saved your life."

He reached over and flicked off the lamp, then stretched out beside Carolyn, wrapping his arms about her.

"When was this?"

"Oh, several years ago."

"Maybe it's better if I don't ask for details."

He kissed her. "You're probably right."

"That was great, Selena," the director said. "All right, everybody. We'll be filming the next scene at two o'clock." He waved his hand at the assembled group and walked off the set.

Wearily Selena slipped a robe over the frothy gown she'd worn for the scene. She'd been expected to be her most seductive, alluring self, and she wondered if being able to perform on a regular basis was worth having to do the type of scenes that were expected of her.

Her character had very little depth—she was merely a foil for the hero, a light comedy relief at times—and the director used her flair for comedy. But oh, how she'd love to have a part with some depth to it—a chance to show another side of her talent, besides her legs and cleavage.

She opened the door to her dressing room and stopped in surprise. Clay sat there waiting for her.

Selena wondered what she would have done without Clay and Carolyn during the six weeks since she'd left the hospital. They'd insisted she convalesce at their home, and they'd kept her entertained while she fought the depression that seemed to have overcome her.

Clay had been on the set earlier, but she hadn't seen him for the past hour and assumed he'd already left.

"How about having lunch with me?" he asked.

Selena felt almost embarrassed that she felt such a need to be alone. But it was no use—she knew she made rotten company.

"Maybe another time. I brought an apple and a piece of cheese to munch on while I reviewed my lines for the afternoon."

Clay's eyes narrowed slightly. "Come on, Selena, you never come in without knowing your lines backward and forward. If you don't want to have lunch with me, why don't you say so?"

"It isn't that, Clay. I...maybe you're right. I probably should get out."

"Great. I'll meet you in the lobby as soon as you change."

But when Selena walked into the lobby, she discovered Clay wasn't alone. A tall, sable-haired man in a well cut, charcoal-gray suit had his back to her, speaking to Clay. When

Clay saw her, he said something to the man, who turned around.

"Adam!"

His smile lit up the lobby, and Selena wondered what happened to the starch in her knees—they suddenly felt as though they could no longer support her.

She held her hand out to him, but instead of shaking it, he pulled her into his arms and kissed her soundly. Pulling back slightly, he whispered, "Hello."

Clay stood watching the two of them with a mischievous grin. After a series of phone calls from Adam, Clay had gone up to the cabin to visit him. They'd spent several hours catching up on the years since they'd last met.

When Clay had finally introduced the subject of Selena, he knew his instincts had been right.

"Is she doing better?" The intensity of Adam's expression had given him away. Clay felt no qualms when he told him she wasn't recovering as well as they'd hoped—which was true. He just didn't tell him his suspicions why.

When Clay invited Adam to come to Los Angeles, Adam explained that he probably wouldn't be going there for several months, not until fall at least. Yet three weeks later he'd called him to say he was in town and asked Clay how to contact Selena. So Clay had brought him to the studio.

"It's good to see you, Adam. I almost didn't recognize you."

"I thought it would be a good idea to see if I could still function in the civilized world, so I came down for a few days."

Her eyes shone. "I'm so glad you did."

Never had Clay felt quite so invisible. "Are you ready? I have reservations for twelve o'clock."

They both looked around at him as though startled to find him there. It was almost impossible for him not to laugh. Each of them had been so careful not to discuss the other one except in the most general terms, but since seeing them together he knew that these two were very much in love. It would be interesting to find out if either of them were aware of it.

The booth was small and Selena felt the length of Adam's thigh against hers. She had no more room to slide away and, at least being honest with herself, admitted that she wanted to stay right there beside him.

His arm brushed against her and she felt it tense. "I'm sorry to crowd you. I'm surprised they sat us here. The table was obviously meant for two people."

She smiled up at him, her eyes dancing. "I'm not complaining."

Her smile hit him like a blow to the stomach. God, how he'd missed her! He'd lost count of the sleepless nights he'd spent, trying to purge her memory from his mind. That smile was one reason he hadn't been successful. "I'm glad to hear it."

"You know, I can't get over how you two managed to meet each other. Adam filled me in on some of the details since you weren't too forthcoming," Clay complained to Selena.

Selena glanced up from her salad. "I thought you said you didn't remember him."

The men exchanged glances. "Well, I've never been that great with names, but I never forget a face!" He leaned back in a relaxed manner and smiled benignly. "How could I possibly forget the man who inspired me to invent Derringer Drake!"

The twin looks of shocked surprise caused him to burst out laughing. It had been worth giving away his closely held secret.

"You mean Adam was—"

"Are you saying that—"

Clay held up his hand. "Wait a minute. One at a time, please." He glanced at Adam. "I'm surprised you didn't recognize yourself."

Selena's gaze fell on Adam as well and her mind quickly reviewed all she'd read. "You mean to tell me that Adam actually lived that sort of life?"

"Let's just say I merely embellished a few facts—changed names and locations to protect the guilty and to avoid a lawsuit, but basically, it was a fairly accurate account of his lifestyle."

"Oh my God," she whispered.

Adam shook his head. "I'll admit I've been impressed with the technical correctness of your writing, but I had no idea you had based your character on a real person." He grinned slightly. "But I know I never had the women around me that Derringer always seems to collect."

"I said you inspired me to write about the character; I had to add a few extras of my own."

"Yes," Selena agreed. "His character's romantic entanglements are all based on Clay's exploits."

"Now cut it out, Selena. You've given me

enough trouble with that kind of remark." He looked at Adam. "When you meet Carolyn you'll understand why I discovered I couldn't be happy without her."

Adam smiled. "I believe I understand the feeling." He didn't look at Selena nor she at him, but her heart started racing at his comment. Was it possible he shared her feelings? She was afraid to hope, but a singing sensation of anticipation swept over her all the same.

"When are you going home?" she asked.

Almost reluctantly, it seemed, Adam turned his head and looked intently into her eyes. "That depends."

"On what?"

"On whether you will see me tonight."

Once again Clay felt invisible as he watched the two across the table from him. He'd never before enjoyed the sensation quite so much.

"I'd like that very much."

"When?"

"About seven, if that's all right."

"That's fine."

The messages going between them had nothing to do with the words they spoke, and Selena could feel her heart slamming against her chest. If she didn't calm down, there was a strong possibility she'd go into cardiac arrest!

"Guess we'd better get back to the studio, right?" Clay asked.

Selena looked around her with wide-open eyes as though surprised to find herself in a crowded room. "Sure."

Adam obligingly slid out of the leather-covered bench seat and helped her to stand.

When they dropped her off at the studio, Adam had the directions to her home tucked safely in his pocket.

She gave them both a wave and hurried into the building. She only hoped she could remember her lines for the afternoon's scenes!

Chapter Ten

Selena decided to have dinner waiting when Adam arrived. She wanted to be alone with him—to talk with him without the noise of others around. Her living room, which had a view of the Pacific Ocean, was washed in warm colors, and she placed a small table in front of the glass wall, overlooking the beach.

Her hands shook so that she could scarcely light the peach-colored candles that matched the place mats on the mahogany table. Dinner was simple—salad and a main dish—as she hadn't had time to prepare anything more elaborate.

When the doorbell rang she was convinced her heart stopped beating. She was getting ir-

ritated with that irresponsible organ that refused to operate in a normal, consistent manner. After taking two slow, deep breaths, she
smoothed the front of the hostess gown she
wore and walked to the door.

Adam had changed to a dark suit and he
look absolutely marvelous. Selena had known
men more handsome, with a distinctive flair
for clothes, and with sparkling personalities
and great charm and wit. But for some reason
this man had stolen her heart, if he but knew
it. And if the darned thing didn't start behaving, she was about ready to get rid of it anyway.

"You're very prompt, Adam, come in."
Was that *her* voice sounding so calm and relaxed? She couldn't believe it. Her years of
training had obviously paid off.

Adam had seen Selena in a dress for the first
time at lunch. The soft, satiny material of the
dress she now wore demurely fell to her toes
but lovingly emphasized every curve of her
body.

He almost groaned at the reaction he was
having just looking at her. The sooner they
found a nice, public restaurant the better. He
paused in the archway of the living room, his

gaze falling on the carefully arranged dinner table.

"Oh, if you don't mind, I thought we might eat here. It will be so much more quiet and give us a chance to talk without interruption."

Exactly what I was afraid of. I need constant interruption or my thoughts are going to get me in trouble before the evening is over. "I didn't want you to go to the trouble to prepare a meal. You had a hard day and I thought you'd want to relax and be waited on for a change."

"My dinner isn't fancy but it was quick. However, if you'd rather eat out—"

"Oh, no. I've never enjoyed crowds that much."

"Neither have I," she murmured.

Oh, hell. How was he going to get through an entire evening alone with her? *You spent several days alone with her.* True, and he'd already used up all of his restraint.

"Would you like a drink?"

"Sounds fine."

"Wine or—"

"Whatever you're having."

She couldn't remember a time when they'd been so polite to each other. She didn't know how to break the tension that had entered the room with him. Should she be honest and admit how much she'd missed him?

Selena poured two glasses of white wine and offered him one, motioning for him to sit down. The view from her living room was spectacular—guaranteed to soothe the most tumultuous case of nerves. As they sat there sipping their wine and gazing at the tranquil scene, Selena could see that Adam was slowly being drawn into that serenity.

"You have a beautiful place here. It's hard for me to understand why you needed to leave it."

Selena smiled. "Perhaps so that I could better appreciate it when I came home."

"I've never told you how sorry I was you were hurt." His eyes seemed to peer deeply into her soul.

She felt as though he knew what she was thinking, so she might as well give voice to it. "Why did you leave?"

He heard the soft hesitancy, the overtone of pain, and recognized for the first time that she was equally involved with him, whether she wanted to be or not. Whether he wanted her to be or not. They might as well face it together.

"I was scared."

"Scared? You? Of what?"

"Of what I was feeling."

They continued to stare at each other and Selena felt the strong surge of feeling he was always able to provoke within her, only this time she didn't fight it. "What were you feeling?"

He shrugged. "As though I had a right to be there, as though you really *were* mine to protect...and love."

"I wanted you to come back so much. I pleaded with Clay to leave me there, but he wouldn't."

"I know. He explained to me the reasoning for transferring you. It made sense."

"Did you ever go back to the hospital?"

"I called. I didn't intend to see you again but I wanted to be sure you were all right. They told me you'd left."

"If you didn't want to see me again, why are you here?"

"I would think that's obvious... I couldn't help myself. I had to see you."

Selena's hand was trembling so, she was afraid of spilling her wine. She carefully set it down on the table beside her, absently noting that Adam had drained his glass and had also set it down.

Taking a deep breath Selena stood up and crossed over to the large, overstuffed chair that Adam occupied and knelt down in front of him. "I'm so glad you did. I've missed you very much." She rested her hand on his knee and felt the muscle tense.

He glanced around the room, then back at her. "After living alone all of this time I can better understand why I could have missed you—your voice, your presence—but I don't quite understand why you've missed me." He gently stroked her hair away from her face and she could feel the slight tremor.

"Because I love you, Adam," she answered softly.

He froze, his expression incredulous. "You what?"

"Is that so surprising?"

He lifted her onto his lap so that he was looking into her eyes from only a few inches away. "Surprising? More like a miracle, Selena," he murmured.

With the most gentle of movements his arms slowly tightened around her, bringing her closer to him. His face was filled with a look of wonder, almost awe, when he lowered his mouth to hers.

Selena felt as though she'd finally come

home because home would always be in Adam's arms. His kiss told her all she needed to know. He'd missed her, he wanted her and he was confused about his feelings.

She gave herself up to the sensations that only Adam seemed to evoke within her. Bells seemed to go off around her every time he kissed her. Then she realized that the noise she heard was the timer going off—her casserole needed to come out of the oven.

Reluctantly she pulled back from him. "Our dinner is ready," she whispered.

"I wonder who was saved by the bell?"

She grinned. "Not you, my friend. I'm going to feed you and lull you into a false sense of security and then—"

"And then what?"

She gracefully stood up, pulling him up beside her. "And then...you'll have to wait and see."

His hand rested lightly on her waist as she stood in the circle of his arms. "I can hardly wait."

Selena escaped to the kitchen and turned off the buzzer. After carefully transferring the casserole into a serving dish, she placed their salads and plates on a large tray and returned to the other room.

Adam stood staring out at the view and she had a moment to study him. He'd removed his jacket and rolled up the sleeves of his shirt. His arms were darkly tanned, a pleasing contrast to the light color of the shirt. It didn't seem to matter what he wore; his clothes became a backdrop to his physique and his personality. Somehow they managed to enhance him.

She wished she were an artist and could draw the strong, smooth lines of his body, showing the strength—and the tenderness— that were there.

He glanced around when she placed the tray on the table. "I'm sorry. I should have offered to help you."

She grinned. "Oh, you helped a great deal—by staying in here. I seem to have trouble concentrating whenever you're around."

"Funny. I have the same complaint about you."

They smiled, and the soft ebb and flow of desire and longing seemed to draw them closer.

"Please sit down," Selena motioned to the table. They sat down across from each other and she lit the candles. The small floral arrangement picked up the peach tones, and

Adam wondered if she knew they matched the soft flush of her cheeks. He enjoyed watching the unflappable Selena Stanford, behaving as an uncertain schoolgirl.

He'd learned a great deal about her since their time together on the mountain. He'd gone out and bought a television set, which meant he also had to invest in a small generator as well as the expensive equipment needed to pick up the signals he needed—just so he could watch her. If he hadn't been in love with her before, seeing her week after week would have done it for him.

She was adorable—unaffected, lighthearted, glamorous, seductive and a rare comedienne. A bundle of talent wrapped in a gorgeous package.

Who wouldn't love her?

She'd told him she loved him, but what did that really mean to her? Her life-style was totally foreign to him. Perhaps she fell in and out of love on a regular basis.

But she's never made love to anyone, he reminded himself. That thought had haunted him for weeks because she'd willingly offered herself to him. Perhaps her feelings for him were special.

That's what he'd come to Los Angeles to find out.

They laughed a great deal over their meal. Adam shared several of Duke's antics with her, and she told him of some of the silliness that took place on the set to release some of the tremendous tension and pressure that was as much a part of the series as the set on which they performed.

They talked about what had happened on the mountain. They talked about sports, and politics and saving the whales. They talked about wars and rumors of wars. They talked about anything—and everything—but themselves.

"Was there a particular reason you came to L.A. at this time, Adam?" she asked while pouring their coffee.

"In a way. There was a man I decided to see who has been trying to contact me for several months."

"Oh?" Did she dare pry?

"He wants me to come to work for him, sort of as a freelance insurance investigator."

"How did he know of you?"

"He said I came highly recommended. It sounds like D.G.'s planning the next stage of my recovery for me—forcing me back into the world."

"Do you think you'll do it?"

He glanced at her over his cup. "Let's just say I'm thinking about it."

She tilted her head slightly. "Would it be possible to coax you into trying it to see if you'd like to do it?"

"Are you volunteering to do the coaxing?" he asked with interest.

"I might be."

The teasing expression slowly left his face and he looked at her intently. "I'm not sure I'm ready to leave my retreat, Selena."

"Will you ever be?"

"I don't know. I know that it was my salvation. Perhaps that's where I need to stay."

"You're the only one who can decide that, Adam."

"Yes. It's only lately that I've discovered it's rather lonely up there without Eve."

"I see. Are you taking applications?"

"Are you applying for the position?"

Selena wondered how she could sound so lighthearted and flippant, when they were talking about something she wanted more than anything she'd ever dreamed of before. Yes, she enjoyed acting, but she'd discovered that without Adam in her life, she didn't feel fulfilled.

But she had commitments—a contract—and right now she couldn't go running off to Eden, no matter how attractive the offer.

Selena stood up and gathered their plates. Adam followed her with the cups and wine glasses into the kitchen. Her lack of a response to his last teasing comment told him all he needed to know. She had her life already established and it did not include him.

Finally he broke the silence. "That was a wonderful meal, Selena."

She glanced over her shoulder while she rinsed off the dishes. "Thank you."

"I know you must be tired. I'd better go so you can get some rest."

She reached over and with studied precision turned off the water. Then she dried her hands carefully on a small hand towel before turning to face him.

"You're going back to the mountains," she stated in a neutral tone.

"Yes."

Walking over to him she rested her palm against his cheek. "I'm so glad I had the chance to get to know you, Adam. You're a very special person."

He slipped his arms around her. "So are you, love."

"Do you suppose we met at the wrong time?" she asked wistfully.

He shook his head. "Not for me. You came into my life at just the right moment." He leaned down and softly kissed her.

"So now we're going to be friends," she whispered painfully.

"Friends? What I'm feeling for you is much stronger than friendship."

"What are you feeling?"

"Such a powerful surge of love that it almost frightens me. I don't understand it."

Selena realized that unless she wanted the nebulous beginning of their relationship to dwindle and die from lack of nourishment, she would have to be the one to force the issue. Otherwise, Adam would walk out of that door and return to his hiding place. She almost panicked. They needed time—time to get used to having the other one as a part of their lives, but how could she gain that time?

"Adam, please don't go."

The quiet intensity in her voice touched a chord of longing deep within him, and he looked down at the beautiful woman in his arms, certain she could feel the trembling of his body. Her eyes were filled with tenderness and a yearning he'd never witnessed before, directed toward him.

What did he have to offer her? Nothing but the broken shell of a man who'd spent too many years alone in too many dangerous situations, who wasn't even sure he could function in the only world she knew. She had come into his life like a bright ray of sunshine lighting the dark tunnel of his mind. How could he consider trying to capture that ray of light? She had too much to offer, too much talent to waste it hidden away with him on his mountaintop, and he didn't have the courage to join her world. Did he have the courage to walk away?

"Selena, we both know it won't work, whatever this is between us."

"It won't work, or you aren't going to give it a chance?"

She stood there in his arms, feeling the tension in his body, and fought for her very life's happiness. She wouldn't give up, not as long as he continued to look at her like a starving man presented with a loaded buffet table, only to be told he couldn't partake of the food.

His impassive tone belied his tortured expression. "It will only make it harder on both of us."

"Will it?"

"I care too much for you to love you, then walk away."

Her arms came up slowly around his neck. "Then don't walk away."

His last coherent thought was, *This isn't fair. She's perfected her abilities to be able to seduce anyone. How can I resist her?*

He knew that he couldn't. A slight groan escaped him while his mouth found hers like a homing device locked on target. She felt so right in his arms, just where she belonged, and he ached with his need for her.

Selena pulled back a few inches and looked up at him, breathless. The smile she gave him was blissful. She began to unfasten his tie.

"Selena…"

"Hmmm?" With agile fingers she opened the buttons of his shirt.

"Are you sure?"

"I've never been more sure of anything in my life." She glanced up at him but couldn't face the burning intensity in his eyes. She dropped her gaze and stared at his belt buckle. *I can't do it,* she admitted to herself. Buttons, yes; belt buckles, uh uh. Television never allowed anything below the belt so she had no experience to fall back on. She glanced at his cuffs and debated about them.

"Selena?"

She could feel the heat in her face. "Hmmm?"

"Look at me." Was that amusement in his voice? Her gaze traveled to his mouth. There was a definite hint of laughter in the slight tilt of his lips.

She forced herself to meet his eyes. His smile widened. "If you're planning my seduction, couldn't you find a more comfortable place than the kitchen?"

The kitchen? Selena glanced around the room in surprise. She'd forgotten that's where they were.

Adam started laughing. "Oh, love, you are priceless. Did you know that?" He picked her up in his arms and walked out of the room. The hallway beckoned to him and he followed it to the open door at the end. Adam paused at the entrance of what was obviously Selena's bedroom.

"This room looks much more comfortable." He allowed her to slide slowly from his arms until her toes touched the floor.

"Now, then," he murmured. "Where were we?"

Selena had been distracted by his bare chest and the fact that she'd been clutched to it. She glanced around the room then back at him.

The love and tenderness in his face made her knees even weaker than before. When his arms came around her she felt as if she were melting all over him.

His kiss was gentle—a promise of the future, but even more than that, it was a promise of *their* future. Selena knew that somehow, in some way, their lives would be worked out together.

She felt the zipper of her gown slide open. Adam carefully pulled it away from her, his expression of awe and anticipation reminiscent of a child at Christmas.

"You are so beautiful," he muttered as though to himself. "And I love you so much."

Once again he lifted her, this time placing her gently in the center of the bed. He stepped back from the bed, quickly discarding the rest of his clothing. His wide, muscled chest beckoned to her and Selena was engulfed in the melting sensation of the physical need to touch and caress him. When he lowered himself to her side, she tenderly brushed the bare expanse of flesh, unafraid of the next step in their relationship. She wanted to belong to Adam, she wanted to be all that he needed or wanted, and she knew she was taking the first step by giving herself to him without reservation.

Adam's tender caresses made Selena briefly wonder who was doing the seducing but decided not to be concerned—the results were what was important. *Loving Adam is what is important.*

With controlled expertise Adam initiated her into the delights of lovemaking. He didn't rush her. Instead he cherished the opportunity to explore and acquaint himself with the vulnerable peaks and hollows that made up the woman he adored.

Hesitantly Selena followed his lead, imitating his soft touch and delicate caress. She found him magnificent without clothes and stroked his taut muscles with fascination.

Selena felt no fear or confusion. She knew that Adam loved her and that out of some misguided sense of chivalry was prepared to walk out of her life—but not if she could help it.

Adam had a sense of unreality about what was happening. Had he spent too many nights dreaming about having her in his arms? Would he wake up to find this, too, was only a dream?

Her light perfume reassured him. Surely dreams didn't come fully equipped with the scent of her. His hands continued their exploration of her body. She felt so good to him.

When he finally possessed her, Selena felt only a momentary discomfort, then was caught up with the new sensations he was evoking. With a tenderness that brought tears to her eyes Adam showed her the world of sensual pleasure. It surrounded them both, creating a universe of love and fulfillment that transcended the decisions they would have to make in order to spend their lives together.

Selena felt that she was still floating high above the clouds when Adam drowsily murmured, "Are you sure you don't want to come back with me?"

She lazily moved her head on his shoulder so she could see his face. "It isn't a question of what I want, I'm afraid. I have a contract to fulfill. There's no way I can get out of it." She didn't want to make any decisions for him. He had to work through his situation for himself. All she could do was offer him her unqualified love.

He kissed her, a leisurely kiss that promised a great deal. "It's going to be a little inconvenient, carrying on a long-distance affair."

Selena felt her heart leap in her chest. Of course. Neither of them had mentioned marriage. She remembered all that he had told her—about his solitary childhood, his need for independence, his lone-wolf life-style. Well, she would have to become so necessary to him, so utterly indispensable, that he would discover his need for her. Was his love for her enough to coax him from his solitary existence? Only time and patience would tell. But she was willing to gamble her future on his eventual capitulation to the strong ties they had already forged together.

Adam needed to learn that she did not intend to tie him down or bind him in any way. He reminded her of a wolf whom she was coaxing from the wild life to a safe, warm refuge. She would have to do it in stages. With a sense of satisfaction she remembered that the wolf mated for life.

She kissed him under the ear. "I'll come up to see you whenever I can, you know that."

He sighed, vaguely discontent with the proposed relationship, but unsure why. "I suppose I could spend some time down here with you," he said slowly.

"Only if that's what you want."

He tightened his arm, pulling her so that she

was sprawled on top of his chest. "You are what I want. I can't seem to get enough of you." He pulled her mouth down to his, his kiss igniting fires that Selena had innocently assumed were banked for the night.

"I love you, Adam," she murmured when he paused, his heart thumping hard against his chest.

His gaze took in her tumbled hair, slightly swollen mouth and love-warmed eyes. "I love you, too," he started to say when his voice broke.

That was all that mattered to Selena. She knew the coming months would be difficult, but she had faith in their love and in their ability to face the future together.

Chapter Eleven

The bright illumination of the summer storm lit up the sky and was immediately followed by a crash of thunder. Selena peered through the sluice of water cascading over the windshield and shook her head.

The storm reminded her of the first time she'd traveled to the mountains, looking for a quiet retreat. In the three years since then, her life had taken a different turn in many respects.

She'd found love in the mountains three years ago—and peace. She'd come to grips with the fact that her life could be whatever she wanted it to be, if she only had the courage to make it so.

Her headlights picked up the curve in the road ahead, and she knew that the road she was looking for branched off around the corner. Selena no longer worried about getting lost—she'd made the trip too many times for that. She sometimes thought she could make the trip with her eyes closed. Each twist and turn had been memorized.

Selena pulled into the area where Adam kept his Jeep and almost cried with disappointment. He wasn't there. She had left a message at his office, saying where she'd be for the next several days, but it was anyone's guess when he'd call in for his messages.

When Adam set out to do something, he became totally involved. When he had decided to open his own office in San Francisco and become a consulting investigator, Selena had encouraged him. It had taken a strong resolve for him to strike out on his own. The trouble with Adam was that he was too good at what he did. The demands made on him were enormous, and he was too conscientious not to give his total concentration to each task he undertook.

She smiled at the thought. She'd been the recipient of his total concentration on numerous occasions and definitely considered the personality trait to be an asset.

Facing the fact that there was no way to get into the cabin without getting soaked, Selena gamely gathered her suitcase and bag and trudged up the hillside.

The cabin bore little resemblance to the original she'd first seen on another dark and rainy night. The main room was now used as a living room, while a kitchen and dining area, two spacious bedrooms and a marvelous modern bathroom had since been added. The covered porch gave relief from the rain, and she gratefully set her belongings down while she fished for the key in her roomy handbag.

After getting the door open, she flipped on a switch, pleased to see that so far they had electricity. Of course with this fierce summer storm there was a good chance they'd lose it, at least for a few hours, but Selena had to admit that she enjoyed the added light.

She had never been able to appreciate fully the earlier cabin's rustic charm. She stepped to the door of the bedroom, again flipping a switch, and smiled. Adam had been here since her last visit.

He constantly amazed her with his neatness. Not that she was messy, but she remembered

having left in a hurry their last time up there
together and had only hastily straightened the
room. Now it was immaculate and included a
card propped up against the mirror with the
words "I love you" printed neatly on it.

Stripping off her soggy clothes, Selena
started running the bath water and tried not to
wonder when Adam might be able to join her.
She had never made any restrictions on him
during their relationship. At times she still felt
as though she'd managed to coax a lone wolf
from the wild. He was tame enough for her,
but she recognized that he would always have
a lack of domesticity—it seemed to have been
left out of his emotional makeup.

She had been aware that Adam had been
uncomfortable with the emotional hold she
had over him, until he discovered she wasn't
going to use it to restrict him. He'd always had
the freedom to come and go in her life at will.

He had come a long way since the first night
he'd made love to her. She had cheerfully bid
him goodbye the next morning, just as though
she were in the habit of seeing him off before
she went to work each day. Then she pro-
ceeded to wait to hear from him. It hadn't
taken long.

He phoned to see if she would meet him in

San Francisco. Without any questions, she had happily agreed and they had spent two days together. Selena refused to bring up the future; instead, she waited for him to choose the subjects they would discuss.

He drove her to a prestigious office building on Saturday. "I've been looking at office space," he began.

"Oh?"

He glanced down at her with a slightly mocking smile. "I thought I'd better find something to do with my time while I'm waiting for you to visit."

"What kind of office are you considering opening?"

He paused, searching for words. "I got the idea when I was talking with the insurance executive in L.A. With my background I could go into insurance investigation work, but I don't care for southern California that much and I'm not at all sure I can take orders from anyone. So I thought about doing free-lance work, maybe hiring myself out as a consultant."

Selena knew what it must have cost him to make such a decision and she knew that her presence in his life had a great deal to do with it. She was touched. Glancing around at the

building, she asked, "Is this where you plan
to set up offices?"

He looked a little uncertain. "That's why I
wanted you to come up. I'd like to show them
to you…get your opinion."

Selena smiled at the memory. She had never
known him to be unsure of himself, but he had
waited for her approval and suggestions before
signing the lease.

The decision had been a sound one. It
hadn't been long until he was inundated with
offers for work.

Six months later, Adam called to see if she
would meet him at the cabin for a long weekend. They had both been busy and had actually
spent very little time together. Just knowing
he was part of her life had been enough for
Selena.

She would never forget that weekend….

She heard Duke barking by the time she was
halfway up the trail. *I wonder how he likes the
confines of the big city.* From the sound of his
bark he was much more in his element up
here, overlooking the rest of the world.

By the time she rounded the corner of the
cabin, the door stood open and Adam was in
the doorway. Instead of stepping back to allow

her to enter, he grabbed her around the waist and pulled her tightly against him.

"My God, but I've missed you!" he muttered into her hair. He slid his thumb under her chin and brought it up so that her mouth was directly below his. "I can't take much more of this." When his lips found hers she was more than ready for him. Her suitcase and purse were forgotten, along with the display of affection being given by Duke. All that mattered was that she was with Adam once again.

His kiss told her more than he ever had—of his love and his passion, of his need for her and his distrust of that need, of his everlastingly independent nature that warred with his desire to spend every day with her.

All she could do was to give him herself, totally, and wait for him to discover that she was no threat to his independence and strength. She didn't intend to take anything away from him—only give of herself.

Slowly he let go of her and absently closed the door behind them. "You look tired."

She laughed. "That's one of the things I really like about you, Adam. I never have to worry about any of your compliments going to my head."

He ignored that. "You've been working too hard."

She shrugged. "Who hasn't? Isn't that the name of the game these days? Work hard and you, too, will become a success?"

"But is it worth it?"

"Good question. Some day I may find an equally good answer and astound both of us."

"Have you eaten?"

"Since when? Yesterday? Yes, I have. Sometime before lunch I think I found a few things to nibble on."

"You need to eat more. You're too thin." He strode to the kitchen area and placed a pot on the stove."

"Thank you, kind sir. You're looking smashing yourself."

He glanced over his shoulder and saw her watching him with amusement while she leaned her hip against the back of the sofa.

"I worry about you," he finally admitted with a sheepish shrug.

"Is that what all of this is about? I thought you were in training as a consultant for one of Elizabeth Arden's make-over salons." She walked around the end of the sofa and sank down with a blissful sigh. "I don't know what it is about this place, but I always feel as though I've returned to nature whenever I come back.''

''You have. You're also breathing fresh air for the first time in months. Be careful you don't get high on it.''

Selena ran her fingers through her hair. ''Oh, don't worry. I brought tanks of smog with me in case I can't handle the pure stuff up here.''

Adam handed her a bowl of what looked to be goulash—it smelled delicious. She needed no encouragement to dive in and enjoy. ''How long can you stay?'' he finally asked, after pouring them both steaming cups of coffee.

''I have to go back Sunday. We're rehearsing all day Monday and Tuesday.''

''Don't you ever get a break?''

''Sure. I had two months off last summer, or have you already forgotten.'' She shook her head. ''How soon we forget,'' she added with a smile. She sipped on her coffee and waited.

It wasn't long in coming. Adam leaned forward, resting his elbows on his knees. ''I've been thinking.''

She refused to comment. His serious demeanor was making her nervous and she knew that whatever she might say would be totally unsuitable for the occasion and probably outrageous as well. Selena was learning to control her unruly tongue.

He glanced at her and she schooled her expression to reveal attentive interest.

"I don't really think this arrangement is going to work."

Her heart bounded into her throat.

"Oh?"

"I've discovered that I want to wake up with you every morning, not just occasional weekends. I'm not satisfied with having an affair with you."

"But I thought that was what you wanted," she responded quietly.

He stared at her in surprise. "I thought it was, too."

"What is it you want?"

He shook his head wearily. "What I want and what we can work out are two different things." He slowly picked up her hand and stroked it. "What I really want, more than anything, is to marry you, but that really wouldn't solve the commuting problem."

It certainly wasn't the most romantic proposal she'd ever heard of, but Selena's heart soared at his words, even though they'd been delivered with a slight frown.

"Would it help you to know that my contract expires in six months?"

"I'm sure they intend to renew it."

"But I don't want to renew it."

Adam drew Selena into his arms. "Oh,
love, don't make sacrifices like that. I never
meant to do that to you."

Selena laughed. "It's hardly a sacrifice. I've
been planning my new career for some time."

"What new career?"

"I've been learning how to write screen-
plays, and Clay tells me I'm getting rather
good at it."

"Are you serious?"

"Yes. I helped write a couple of the recent
episodes on our series and they went over very
well. Clay assures me I have enough talent to
make it, if I'd prefer that to acting."

"Do you?"

"I think so. I really do. But even more im-
portantly, I can write anywhere, even in San
Francisco or up here."

"You mean you'd actually consider marrying me?"

She grinned. "I've never had any intentions
of not marrying you. My intentions have always been honorable, if, perhaps, a little un-
orthodox." She threw her arms around his

neck. "I was beginning to wonder if you were *ever* going to ask!"

"Oh, my love, how was I ever so fortunate to find you?"

"Actually, I believe it was the other way around...but there's no reason to quibble over it."

For the past two years Selena had made her home in San Francisco, in the condominium Adam had purchased. She'd just spent the past three days in Los Angeles at a writers' conference concerning a new series. Adam had been called out of town before she left so that it had been almost a week since they'd seen each other, a week that had seemed more like a lifetime to her.

She glanced around the room with pride. She'd enjoyed helping him remodel his mountain retreat and was delighted with his response to her suggestions. He'd finally mellowed in the years they'd been together and she'd also found what she wanted to do with the rest of her life. She'd been surprised to discover talents she'd never known existed— a depth she'd never attempted to plumb. And now it looked as though it was going to pay off.

If only Adam would get there so she could share her latest news!

Selena was sound asleep when Adam stepped into the bedroom. She'd left the bathroom night-light on, and he paused beside the bed to enjoy the sight of her.

She was still the most gorgeous woman he knew—and she was beautiful all the way through. She'd brought a richness and fullness to his life that he'd never imagined experiencing.

He hadn't gotten her message until late and should have gotten some sleep before making the trip, but he couldn't wait to see her. He decided to shower, hoping to relax the tired muscles in his neck and shoulders.

I'm working too hard and I don't even know why. He stepped under the hot, steamy water and sighed with pleasure. Selena had been right. They could enjoy the retreat just as well with hot and cold running water.

What a difference she'd made in his life. He sometimes felt as though his life before they'd met had been someone else's. She'd added a special dimension to his existence.

He shut off the water and grabbed a towel. After briskly drying himself he entered the bedroom once again. She hadn't moved. Lifting the covers he slid in beside her.

"Adam?"

"Who else were you expecting?" he whispered.

He heard her drowsy chuckle. "What time is it?"

"After two."

She moved into his arms and sighed. "I've missed you so much. Remind me not to ever go away again."

"I knew that sooner or later my unusual charm would work its magic and you'd never be able to escape me."

Selena settled on his shoulder with a nod. "That's what did it, all right. Your magical charms." She drifted off to sleep once again.

For the first time since she'd left, Adam relaxed and fell into a restful sleep. They were where they belonged—in each other's arms.

Selena came awake slowly, basking in the warmth of the muscular body alongside her. Adam stroked her soft curves, his hand sliding from her shoulder to the indentation of her waist, then slowly following the contour of her slim hips.

Her eyes opened and she feasted on the

view of Adam's broad, muscular chest. She couldn't resist running her fingers over the wide expanse.

"Good morning," he murmured, kissing her.

"It certainly is," she agreed, increasing the pressure of her mouth on his.

Adam never seemed to get tired of holding Selena, making love to her, enjoying her. He wanted to absorb her through his pores, become one with her. While their kisses deepened he pulled her on top of him, her long blond hair making a veil around his head.

With the ease of two people who know how to please each other, they shared the depths of their feelings in various, pleasurable ways. Their mutual cries of release echoed throughout the cabin and Selena limply slid to one side of him.

Adam stroked her hair away from her face.

"How was Los Angeles?"

"Hot...crowded...but well worth the trip."

He heard the note of excitement in her voice. "What happened?"

"I was offered a position as one of the writers on a new series."

"That's marvelous. No doubt you said yes."

She smiled. "Actually, I did have some conditions. I'm not going to move back down there."

"And they agreed?"

"Yes. One of the nice things about the electronic age is being able to hook up computers. I'll send my scripts and revisions over the phone."

"I'm proud of you."

"Thank you. I'm rather pleased myself."

Adam shifted, making sure her body fit snugly against him. "I'm thinking about cutting back, myself. Would you mind having me around home more often?"

Selena's eyes blinked open in surprise. "Are you serious?"

"I've never been more serious in my life. I realized coming up here that I've been pushing myself, trying to prove something—I don't know what, exactly. Perhaps I wanted to prove to myself that I could make it in the so-called civilized world. Well, I've done that. But you're more important to me than anything else and I miss you when I have to be gone."

"Oh, Adam, I've missed you, too, but I didn't want to give you the impression I'd be a clinging wife."

He laughed. "You? Clinging? About the

only clinging I've managed to coax out of you is here in bed.''

"I just wasn't sure you wanted much of a domestic scene."

He stretched and sighed with sensuous pleasure. "Oh, I don't know. I think I'm becoming downright attached to a life of domesticity."

"I'm so glad to hear it. I was a little concerned about how to tell you my other bit of news."

He leaned up on his elbows to see her expression. She looked a little apprehensive. "What is it?"

She hedged. "Well, you know how Clay and Carolyn have been teasing us about providing a playmate for Adrienne—"

"So you want to start a family, is that it? Why would you think I'd mind? I haven't said anything because I knew your career was important to you and I didn't want to push you into anything you weren't ready for."

She slipped her arms around his neck and gave him a fierce hug. "Well, ready or not, it looks like our family is on its way." She pulled back and studied his dear, familiar face with love.

Adam felt that he could warm himself by

the glow on her face. There was no denying Selena's sincerity. She wanted their baby.

He couldn't help wondering how Duke would handle the new arrival.

Carolyn and Selena sat watching their offspring with maternal pride and amusement. Five-year-old Adrienne was trying to keep the eleven-month-old twins off Duke but was having little success. Duke, showing the patience and fortitude of a saint, relaxed regally in the shade on the Kenniwick lawn, while Timothy and Tricia crawled and tumbled over him as if he were a mountain.

"He's really great with kids, isn't he?" Carolyn marveled.

Selena nodded. "I'm always amazed to watch him with them. You know, they learned to walk by hanging onto his side. I got some marvelous pictures of him strolling across the living room, a twin on each side. The expression on his face was priceless."

Carolyn glanced at the slender woman next to her. "You amaze me. It's hard to believe you ever were large enough to carry twins."

Selena grinned. "Oh, but I was. That was an experience, all right."

"I think Adam was in shock for a week

when the doctor told you there were going to be two."

"Oh, he adjusted all right. Have you told Clay your news?"

Carolyn giggled. "I didn't have to. Ever since you managed to catch up and pass us in the family division, he's been eager to have another one."

"Who would ever have believed those two would be such proud fathers and doting husbands?" Selena mused. "I can think of no two people who would be less likely prospects than Clay and Adam."

"Yes, but we knew, didn't we?"

"Let's just say I hoped. You really think Adam is happy?"

"Disgustingly so. He carries the twins with him everywhere he goes like a couple of cuddly bookends."

Selena smiled. He was very good with them—patient, loving and very gentle. No one seeing him now would ever believe he had inspired the character of Derringer Drake.

She caught a movement out of her eye and turned her head. Adam stood in the doorway of the house, watching her, his heart in his eyes. Yes, he was no longer the man she'd met living alone on a mountaintop, refusing to face the world.

Her lone wolf had found his home.

*   *   *   *   *

WAYS TO *UNEXPECTEDLY* MEET MR. RIGHT:

♡ Go out with the sexy-sounding stranger
  your daughter secretly set you up with
  through a personal ad.

♡ RSVP yes to a wedding invitation—soon
  it might be your turn to say "I do!"

♡ Receive a marriage proposal by mail—
  from a man you've never met....

These are just a few of the unexpected
ways that written communication
leads to love in Silhouette Yours Truly.

Each month, look for two fast-paced, fun and
flirtatious Yours Truly novels
(with entertaining treats and sneak previews
in the back pages) by some of your favorite
authors—and some who are sure to
become favorites.

YOURS TRULY™:
Love—when you least expect it!

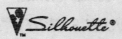

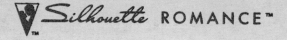
Silhouette ROMANCE™

What's a single dad to do when he needs a wife by next Thursday?

Who's a confirmed bachelor to call when he finds a baby on his doorstep?

How does a plain Jane in love with her gorgeous boss get him to notice her?

From classic love stories to romantic comedies to emotional heart tuggers, **Silhouette Romance** offers six irresistible novels every month by some of your favorite authors! Such as...beloved bestsellers **Diana Palmer, Annette Broadrick, Suzanne Carey, Elizabeth August** and **Marie Ferrarella,** to name just a few—and some sure to become favorites!

Fabulous Fathers...Bundles of Joy...Miniseries... Months of blushing brides and convenient weddings... Holiday celebrations... You'll find all this and much more in **Silhouette Romance**—always emotional, always enjoyable, always about love!

Silhouette

S P E C I A L   E D I T I O N

™

SPECIAL EDITION

Stories of love and life, these powerful
novels are tales that you can identify with—
romances with "something special" added
in!

Fall in love with the stories of authors such
as **Nora Roberts, Diana Palmer, Ginna Gray**
and many more of your special favorites—as
well as wonderful new voices!

Special Edition brings you
entertainment for the heart!

SSE-GEN

SILHOUETTE® Desire®

Do you want...

Dangerously handsome heroes

Evocative, everlasting love stories

Sizzling and tantalizing sensuality

Incredibly sexy miniseries like **MAN OF THE MONTH**

Red-hot romance

Enticing entertainment that can't be beat!

You'll find all of this, and much *more* each and every month in **SILHOUETTE DESIRE**. Don't miss these unforgettable love stories by some of romance's hottest authors. Silhouette Desire—where your fantasies will always come true....

DES-GEN